'Why don't you join me in a fresh cup of coffee?'

Nick smiled as he delivered his invitation, and if he'd been good-looking before he was drop-dead gorgeous now. He had the widest, most genuine grin Rosie could ever remember seeing. It was the smile of someone who smiled often, and her automatic response was to smile back. His whole face lit up and his blue-grey eyes sparkled.

Rosie was tempted to accept his invitation, but for a whole host of reasons she really couldn't. 'Thanks, but we really need to get home. We're very late as it is.'

Nick relaxed his grip, letting her hand go, and only then was Rosie able to get her legs working. She knew she was going to regret walking away. The most incredible-looking man, who seemed decent to boot, had asked her for a coffee and she couldn't accept?

Had she let a once-in-a-lifetime opportunity slide through her grasp?

But she'd done the right thing by the children and said no. Her focus had to be the twins. Following the recent death of their parents, their welfare came first. She owed it to them to let nothing distract her.

And Rosie had a strong feeling a cup of coffee with Nick would have provided her with far too many distractions that she was in no way equipped to deal with.

Dear Reader

Starting a new book is always an exciting adventure—not least because stories generate their own momentum as they unfold. Careful planning and initial ideas get tossed aside helter-skelter as the story gathers a pace all its own.

So it was with my new book, WANTED: A FATHER FOR HER TWINS. I knew all about Rosie Jefferson when I started to tell her story. Then she took me on a few detours I hadn't expected.

I should really have expected that, though, because we never know how we're going to react to events until they happen. So of course Rosie is going to have something to say—especially since she's been tossed some pretty huge curve-balls in the weeks before we meet her.

One thing I was always certain about was that Nick Masters, a gorgeous, driven doctor from New Zealand, is made for Rosie. The timing, though, couldn't be worse for either of them. As their lives get ever more complicated, can they clear all the hurdles and find a way to be together?

I can't tell you that—not yet—but I can tell you that Nick, like Rosie, also has his own plans for dealing with the challenges they face. These two have a lot to say for themselves!

I've loved going on this journey with Nick and Rosie. Or should I say I've loved being taken on this adventure by them? Whichever way, I hope you enjoy the myriad twists and turns as their story unfolds. And I hope the twists and turns life brings you are much smoother, with happy endings for all.

With love

Emily Forbes

WANTED:
A FATHER
FOR HER TWINS

BY
EMILY FORBES

All th[...] [...]ave no exist[...] [...]de the imagination
of the [...] and have no [...] whatever to [...] one bearing the
same [...] [...]ng are not even distantly [...] to [...]
indiv[...] [...] in any way to anyone, and all the incidents are
pure [...]

All F[...] [...] and includes the right of repro[...] in whole or
in pa[...] in any form. This edition is published by arrangement with
Harl[...]uin Enterprises II B.V./S.à.r.l. The text of this publication or
any p[...] [...]eof may not be reproduced or transmitted in any form
or by any means, electronic or mechanical, including photocopying,
recording, storage in an information retrieval system, or otherwise,
without the written permission of the publisher.

® and TM are trademarks owned and used by the trademark owner
and/or its licensee. Trademarks marked with ® are registered with the
United Kingdom Patent Office and/or the Office for Harmonisation in
the Internal Market and in other countries.

First published in Great Britain 2009
Harlequin Mills & Boon Limited,
Eton House, 18-24 Paradise Road, Richmond, Surrey TW9 1SR

© Emily Forbes 2009

ISBN: 978 0 263 20937 2

Set in Times Roman 10¼ on 11¾ pt
15-0809-56724

Harlequin Mills & Boon policy is to use papers that are natural,
renewable and recyclable products and made from wood grown in
sustainable forests. The logging and manufacturing process conform
to the legal environmental regulations of the country of origin.

Printed and bound in Great Britain
by CPI Antony Rowe, Chippenham, Wiltshire

Emily Forbes is the pseudonym of two sisters who share both a passion for writing and a life-long love of reading. Beyond books and their families, their interests include cooking, languages, the arts, playing the piano, netball, as well as an addiction to travel—armchair travel is fine, but anything involving a plane ticket is better. Home for both is South Australia, where they live three minutes apart with their husbands and five young children. With backgrounds in business administration, law, arts, clinical psychology and physiotherapy they have worked in many areas between them. This past professional experience adds to their writing in many ways: legal dilemmas, psychological ordeals and business scandals are all intermeshed with the medical settings of their stories. And, since nothing could ever be as delicious as spending their days telling the stories of gorgeous heroes and spirited heroines, they are eternally grateful that their mutual dream of writing for a living came true.

They would love you to visit and keep up to date with current news and future releases at the blog of the Medical™ Romance authors, 'Love is the Best Medicine', at http://medicalromance.blogspot.com

Recent titles by the same author:

THE PLAYBOY FIREFIGHTER'S PROPOSAL
EMERGENCY: WIFE NEEDED
WEDDING AT PELICAN BEACH
THE SURGEON'S LONGED-FOR BRIDE

There are lots of essentials in a girl's life.
No doubt love scores top position on most women's
lists, but I suspect friendship is right up there for
most of us, too. And there's no friendship quite like
the relationship shared with girlfriends. Sorrows that
require chocolate, successes that demand champagne,
laughter and tears all combine to create a tapestry of
'Do you remember?' moments that, woven together,
make the bond with our female friends so remarkable.

And so, to my beautiful, wonderful, kaleidoscope-
tapestry of girlfriends, thank you for your friendship.
It means more than you know. And to Helen, Ali,
Manda and Anne, a special thank you for your
unwavering support and encouragement.
And while I hope sorrows are few and far between,
there's always chocolate in my cupboard
and a place on my couch for each of you.

This one's for the girls!

CHAPTER ONE

THIS is a perfect moment.

The thought surprised Rosie as she sat on the sparkling gold sands of Bondi Beach, looking out over the clear blue water.

It surprised her because, only a moment before, she'd been reflecting on the one-hundred-and-eighty-degree turn her life had pivoted through two months ago, and every day since: the loss of her beloved brother and sister-in-law; her instant transformation from aunt to the guardian of her twin eight-year-old nephew and niece; the break-up with Philip; the consequent move from Canberra back to Sydney. Since then, she'd been in shock, grief-stricken and feeling like she'd never get on top of her new life.

Yet, sitting here, with the morning sun warming her face, in her first quiet moment that week, she had a brief glimmer of hope that things might somehow work out okay. She picked up a handful of sand and let it trickle slowly through her fingers. The top inch of sand was warm. A little deeper, where the sun's rays hadn't yet penetrated, the sand was cool and damp against her skin.

Another glorious summer day lay ahead. Later on, the beach would be crowded. Right now, it was relatively empty and it didn't take long to scan the beach to check her niece's whereabouts. The junior surf lifesavers had come out of the water and were packing equipment away, Lucy among them. Rosie stood, shaking the sand off her sundress, and walked along the beach towards the group.

'How did you go this morning, Luce?' Her niece had bounded up to her, still full of her usual energy.

'I got a personal best time for the sand sprint. Did you see me?'

'I was watching but you were going so fast you were just a blur!' Rosie hugged the little girl, pulling her into her side. Lucy chatted non-stop as they climbed the path leading from the beach to the esplanade, only pausing for breath once she had her usual post-training Sunday milkshake in hand.

Coming out of Marie's Milk Bar, Rosie nearly tripped over a small dog that dashed past the entrance. She stopped suddenly and felt Lucy bump into her back. A young boy ran past, calling out to the dog. The dog had no intention of obeying and dashed out into the road.

She could see disaster unfolding in front of her.

'Stop!' she yelled, but the boy neither paused nor looked as he chased the animal. Rosie watched with horror as a car swerved sharply to the left to miss the dog, colliding instead with the child.

The car wasn't travelling quickly, the esplanade was too narrow and too busy for that, but it still struck the boy with enough force to send him spinning up into the air before he crashed to the bitumen.

Traffic came to a stop and the hum of dozens of conversations ceased as people processed what had just happened. For a brief moment there was silence before voices began again and witnesses and bystanders swarmed onto the road.

'Wait here,' Rosie said to Lucy, handing over her take-away latte before joining the gathering crowd.

'I'm a doctor.' Rosie raised her voice as she pushed her way through the throng. 'Let me through.'

The driver, a young female, emerged from the car, shaky and pale. 'I didn't see him, I didn't have time to stop.'

'Someone call an ambulance and get this woman to sit down.' The woman would be in shock. Rosie doubted she was injured but, if she was, her injuries would need to wait. The priority was the boy.

He was lying in a crumpled heap on the road, blood spilling from a gash on his head. The car that had hit him was protecting them both from the traffic and Rosie didn't think they were in any immediate danger from that angle. She knelt down beside the child. He was breathing but his eyes were closed. Was he conscious? She gently shook his shoulder, asking him if he could hear her. There was no response.

'Can I help?' Rosie felt, rather than saw, a man crouch down beside her. She didn't look up from her examination of the little boy, but she didn't need to look up to know the man was from New Zealand. The inflection on his vowels told her that. 'I'm a doctor.'

'Thanks.' She also didn't have to look up to know he was tall, and together with the quiet, calm confidence in his voice, it made his presence even more reassuring. 'He's breathing but unconscious.'

'Was there anyone with him? Does anyone know his name?'

Lucy appeared by Rosie's side, cradling the runaway dog in her arms. 'Rosie, it's Matt. From school. Do you want me to get his mum?'

Rosie didn't want to think about how, or where, Lucy had cornered the dog, but she would like to see Matt's mum. She glanced up at her skinny-legged niece, her knees covered in bits of grass and sand. 'Is she here?'

'I don't think so but I know where they live.'

Sending Lucy off on her own wasn't an option. 'Maybe we can ring her?'

'I'll do it.' Marie from the milk bar was standing behind Lucy.

'Thanks.' Rosie nodded at the woman. 'Go with Marie, Luce, and see if you can reach Matt's mum.'

'The ambulance is on its way.' Someone from the crowd passed this information on.

'Matt, can you hear me? Matt?' The other doctor was talking and Rosie turned back to the boy, relieved to find his eyes were now open. 'Hi, there, mate. Lie still, you've had a tussle with a car. My name's Nick, I'm a doctor, and I'm just going to check a few things out. This is…'

He paused and Rosie knew he was waiting for her response. She looked at him properly for the first time and, as their eyes met, she felt a bolt of attraction so strong it made her catch her breath. What an incongruous reaction, she thought as she managed to answer, 'Rosie.' Her voice came out as a whisper.

'She's a doctor too.'

Rosie had to force herself to concentrate as they both turned their attention back to Matt. She applied pressure to the gash in Matt's head, using a clean beach towel from her bag, and took his pulse with her other hand.

'Where does it hurt?' Nick asked.

'My arm and my leg.' His right leg was bloodied and there was already significant swelling around his knee.

'Can you wriggle your toes?'

Matt could move his toes but moving his foot seemed to cause him pain. Rosie watched as Nick ran his large hands gently over Matt's leg, feeling for any major trauma. Matt had probably sustained a fractured fibula and possibly even tibia but, as his leg was still straight, Rosie suspected it wasn't too bad. As she listened to Nick's examination she couldn't help but catch glimpses of him whilst checking her watch and timing Matt's pulse.

His jaw was strong, slightly square in shape without being heavy, and darkened by a shadow of a beard, as if he hadn't shaved for a day or two. He had fabulous cheekbones, a narrow nose, not too big and not too small, and the fullest lips she'd ever seen on a man, a perfect cupid's bow. The masculine strength of his facial bone structure saved his nose and mouth from looking almost too perfect. His dark hair was thick and wavy with a cowlick at the front.

He squatted beside Rosie, his shoulders higher than hers, and she guessed he was taller than she was by several inches, no mean feat when she was five feet ten inches. His limbs were long and lean and he looked in good physical shape. She was glad she was the one applying pressure to the wound, leaving her free to soak in his image. Not that she was interested in him, of course. She didn't even have time to put the washing away, so how would she ever have time to meet another man? But a girl would have to be comatose not to appreciate pure aesthetic male beauty when she was staring right at it.

'How about your fingers?' Nick asked the boy.

Matt was clutching his right arm, trying to keep it immobile, but managed to wriggle his fingers.

'Can you tell me what day it is?'

'Friday?'

The uncertainty in Matt's reply told them what they needed to know. There was no need to tell him it was Sunday but he obviously had concussion.

'Matt, you've broken your arm and your leg, I'll need you to keep lying as still as you can for a little bit longer,' Nick instructed.

Rosie heard the wail of an ambulance siren in the distance and as she tilted her head to listen to make sure it was coming closer, she saw Marie and Lucy returning. Marie gave her a thumbs-up signal.

Rosie deliberately trained her eyes on Matt as she spoke, not willing to risk losing her breath again if she accidentally sneaked a glance at her temporary colleague. 'Your mum is on her way and I'll wait with you until the ambulance gets here. It will take you and your mum to the hospital.' Rosie kept hold of Matt's good hand while she kept the pressure on his head wound with her other hand. A single tear rolled down his cheek. 'It'll be okay, Matt. You're being very brave.'

Nick stood up, stretching his legs and distracting Rosie. He was wearing a T-shirt and boardshorts that showed off tanned, muscular calves. Where had he been when the accident happened? Had he just been for a swim? She looked up further. His hair was clean and dry so perhaps he was just on his way to the beach. As she watched, he ran his hand through the front of his hair, pushing it off his face from where it fell from the cowlick. He really was striking.

A siren's 'whoop, whoop' pierced the air as the ambulance manoeuvred the final distance through the traffic. In the next moment Matt's mother arrived and Rosie went to comfort her and explain the situation while Nick filled the paramedics in.

The paramedics did their checks, popped a cervical brace around Matt's neck as a precaution, stabilised his arm and splinted his leg before rolling him onto the stretcher. In a few minutes Matt and his mother were being whisked off to hospital.

Just like that, everything was back to normal, the crowd was dispersing, Marie had returned to her shop and the traffic was flowing freely again. The car that had hit Matt had been moved to the side of the road and the driver was giving her statement to a policeman. There was a sense of anticlimax. Only she, Lucy and Nick stood on the edge of the pavement. Despite being a doctor, she'd never been at the scene of an accident before. What happened next? Should she thank Nick for his help or simply say goodbye? As she stood there, pondering the dilemma, Lucy started asking questions, breaking the silence.

She expected Nick to head straight off but he stayed put, seemingly content to listen to her confident, chatty niece, so different from her twin. There didn't seem to be anybody waiting for him. Maybe he was as uncertain of the etiquette of beachside medical emergencies as she was? She smiled at the idea; uncertainty was not a quality that fitted this man.

'Thanks for your help, Nick.' She met his gaze, still smiling. 'Don't let us hold you up.'

'You're not.' He returned her smile and his was hands-down the most adorable, warming grin she'd ever been treated to. If he'd been good-looking before, he was drop-dead gorgeous now, his whole face lit up, his blue-grey eyes sparkling. 'I've only got a half-drunk cup of coffee to get back to and it'll be cold by now. Join me for a fresh cup.' He spread his hands wide to include them both and Lucy immediately took a step closer to him. His was clearly a charm with cross-generational power.

She was tempted to accept his invitation, purely so she had an excuse to sit and look at him for a bit longer, but, for a whole host of reasons, she really couldn't't. 'Thanks, but we really need to get home. We're late as it is.' She didn't have to pretend polite regret, her whole body was thrumming with a desire to go with him. A wave of disappointment slammed over her, leaving her reeling.

He nodded, accepting her decision, cocking his head to the side to indicate he was sorry they couldn't stay. Then Lucy tugged on his hand and pulled him down to her. He stooped to hear her and as the pair of them chatted, Rosie simply stared at the moment of realisation she'd just had.

If she'd been able to, she'd go with him anywhere, wherever he took her. She wouldn't even have asked. She, who'd never been spontaneous, would have gone with a perfect stranger, no questions asked. She, who was cast in the perfect mould of a careful, methodical, responsible planner, would have tossed all that aside and simply held out her hand for him to take. But aunts responsible for the well-being of young twins didn't have the luxury of being spontaneous, even if it had been in her to do so. It wasn't in the job description of being the perfect guardian.

She looked from the top of Lucy's blonde head to Nick's dark one and back again, visually tracing his profile as he laughed at something Lucy was saying. Then he straightened up and met her gaze, catching her out.

'Th-thanks again for your h-help,' she stammered, sure he'd
see the inconsistency between her words and her desires, tem-
porarily blind-sided by the discovery of a whole new side to
herself. A side that, had circumstances been different, would
have let him take her hand and take her anywhere, do anything,
and have her begging for more. 'I really did appreciate not
dealing with that on my own.'

'Don't mention it. Perhaps we'll bump into each other again
under better circumstances.' He didn't seem to notice her confusion, her stammer or what she was sure was a wild look in
her eyes. He held out his hand and Rosie took it. His grip was
warm and firm, not too soft, not too strong. But more than that,
there was a connection, just as she'd already known there
would be, as though his touch had pushed a button in her palm.
A button that went straight to her chest, making her heartbeat
faster and her breathing more shallow. The connection travelled
further, to the pit of her stomach, as though a thousand butter-
flies were there, fluttering madly towards an impossible escape.

She stood, her hand in Nick's, completely unable to move
away until Lucy, obviously tired of waiting now she no longer
had Nick's attention, said, 'Come on, Rosie, we need to drop
Matt's dog off at his house on the way.'

It was only then that Rosie noticed Lucy was still holding the
little white bundle of trouble. Somehow the dog had managed
to come through the whole drama completely unscathed.

'Right, of course,' she said to her niece. 'Goodbye, Nick.'
'Bye, Rosie.'

Nick relaxed his grip, letting her hand go, and only then was
Rosie able to get her legs working, although she was aware of
her muscles fighting every step, protesting her departure. With
every instinct screaming at her to stay, she followed Lucy and
left Nick standing alone behind her.

Was walking away going to be a whole new source of regret?
She knew the answer already. The most incredible-looking man,

who seemed kind and decent to boot, had asked her for a coffee and she didn't have enough of a life that she could accept?

Balance.

She was missing any sort of balance. She glanced at Lucy, who was swinging on her hand, chirping away about her morning. She loved these two children, she had no qualms or doubts about taking care of them, but she'd scarcely drawn breath these last weeks. That's all it was, that was all that lay behind her reaction. It made no sense to be overcome by fantasies of disappearing over the horizon with a perfect stranger. It was only because the equilibrium in her life right now was non-existent, otherwise, she'd have noticed Nick was good-looking but not given it another thought.

And yet, even with that perfectly rational explanation ringing in her ears, she had to struggle to leave.

'We have to go down this street,' Lucy told her as they reached the corner.

Rosie stopped just short of the corner, which loomed like the point of no return in front of her. If she continued into the side street, would Nick be gone for ever? She hesitated. They didn't really have to go straight home. They could go back. Lucy liked him, too. Her niece would enjoy a few more minutes with Nick as much as Rosie would, so it wasn't just her own out-of-character desire to run back to Nick that was causing her to linger on the corner. Right?

If Nick was watching them, she'd go back and have a coffee. If not, she'd keep going.

Turning around, she saw him talking to the policeman, obviously giving his version of events. He was concentrating on the conversation, his face in profile. He wasn't looking in her direction. No doubt she was already far from his mind and she wouldn't be given so much as another brief thought.

Rosie turned the corner, her disappointment acute.

Had she let a once-in-a-lifetime opportunity slide through

her grasp? Or was it really only a wake-up call to sort her new life out better?

She sighed and ruffled Lucy's damp hair. He'd asked her for a coffee, nothing more than that.

None of it mattered anyway. She'd done the right thing by the children. She hadn't followed the heady pull towards Nick. Sure, maybe that had only been by default but she'd stayed true to her commitment. Her focus was the twins. Her priority was solely their welfare and she wouldn't be distracted.

A cup of coffee with Nick would have provided her with far too many distractions. Distractions she at least had enough common sense left to know she was in no way equipped to deal with.

Nick glanced up from his conversation with the policeman just as Rosie turned the corner. Good-looking women were a dime a dozen in Bondi but there was something about this one… What was it? Her general appearance wasn't dissimilar to hundreds of other women who frequented Sydney beaches, slim, tall and blonde. It was something else telling him she was different.

She seemed a little misplaced in Bondi, was that it? Even the backpackers blended into the crowd but Rosie seemed almost to stand apart from everyone else.

And what about the little girl with her? Rosie had no rings on her fingers and the girl had called her by her name, not Mum. She was a trained doctor so he guessed she wasn't the au pair. Maybe Rosie was the partner of the girl's dad? It seemed the most likely scenario. Pity, he would have liked to have had a coffee with her and he'd been hoping when he looked up she might have changed her mind and been heading back to him.

'One last thing—'

The policeman had stopped scribbling in his pad and Nick had to turn his attention back to him.

Maybe he and Rosie would bump into each other again if she lived around here.

Then again, he told himself as he finished with the policeman and headed down to the beach for his swim, any involvement with a woman was the last thing on his to-do list right now. She was the first woman he'd met in a long time to really pique his interest and he wasn't sure a coffee would sufficiently cool that interest.

There were places and times for everything in life. He didn't doubt there would come a time and a place for a woman in his life again one day.

But right now wasn't the time. Or the place.

Then how to explain this lingering feeling that a chance encounter on the beach might have shown him the woman?

Madness. He'd taken temporary leave of his senses due to…work stress? That was it. Work stress, life stress. So naturally his body wanted some female distraction, right at the very time he least needed it, when he was so close to finally realising his goals.

He waded into the waves, the cool of the sea hitting his shins before he dived in, striking out for his ritual Sunday swim. The water, slick on his skin, was as stimulating as it always was.

Pushing himself to go harder, faster, he willed the water to wash away the image of a certain woman from his mind.

Any form of temptation was madness. And that's all this was. Nothing more.

CHAPTER TWO

LUCY raced inside, eager to tell her brother all the morning's news, while Rosie headed for the kitchen, where her mother was doing the last of the breakfast dishes.

'What happened? Are you all right?'

Rosie followed her mother's gaze, looking down at her sundress that had started the day clean and white but was now covered in blood and dirt.

'I'm fine. It's not my blood. There was an accident, a pedestrian was hit, a boy from Lucy's school.' Rosie pulled out a kitchen stool and collapsed onto it. She should probably take over the dishes from her mum but she didn't have the energy.

'Is he okay?'

'Some broken bones but he'll be fine. It was a bit crazy.'

'I'll put the kettle on, you look like you could use a cup of tea.'

The old ritual of a cup of tea as a cure-all. Funnily enough, it did always seem to help. Maybe because it made you stop and catch your breath? Then again, in the two months since her brother and sister-in-law had died, she'd had so many cups of tea she sometimes felt she was one big tea bag herself.

Half-heartedly, she started sorting through the stack of mail, including her own redirected post, that had been dumped in a teetering pile on the kitchen bench. One more task that seemed to be getting away from her, one more task she started on routinely but never completed. Was that a key part of the definition of parenthood? She was starting to wonder.

Her mum slid a cup of tea over the counter. 'Ally phoned while you were out, she said something about going out tonight. Do you need me to watch the children?'

'Thanks, but no. I wasn't planning on going.'

'Are you sure? It'd do you good.'

'What do you mean?' Rosie put aside the mail.

'How many times have you been out since you moved back to Sydney? Twice? For coffee with Ally, nothing more at my count.'

She shrugged. 'I'm often out.'

Her mum pushed a strand of hair out of her face and shook her head. 'Going to the supermarket and dropping the twins at school doesn't count. You need to see your friends and it's not good for you or the children if you spend all your time with them.'

'I want them to know I'm here for them, that they're not alone.'

'They know that, sweetheart.'

'Do they? I know they worry when I go out in the car without them. The last time they saw their parents was as they were driving off for their weekend away. They haven't expressed that, but it's what they're thinking about, it's in their eyes,' Rosie explained.

'I understand what you're saying but you can't let that make you a hermit,' her mother pointed out.

'The twins need time, especially Charlie. So far we've somehow managed to stop his mutism worsening because at least he's still talking to our immediate family, but if he starts to doubt he's safe with me, what then? And I need time, too. For one thing, I'm not sure how, or if, my old life and my new life can coexist. I'm just trying to give myself space to fit the pieces together.'

'Space is one thing, shutting friends out is another,' her mother insisted.

'Mum, I'm not intentionally doing that. To be honest, as pathetic as it sounds, I don't have the energy to get dressed and make conversation.' She could have added that she didn't have anything to make conversation about. No one she knew had children. Right now, that was all she had to talk about. When had she last managed to stay awake to see the end of a TV show? Ditto for reading. She'd been on the same chapter of the same book for over three weeks. Within minutes of settling down, she nodded off. Night after night.

A basket of washing waited on the steps. Sure, it was clean, but there was more waiting in the laundry. Newspapers for re-cycling were lying by the back door and Lucy's half-finished school project was scattered over an entire end of the kitchen table. Everywhere Rosie looked there were half-completed tasks, testament to her difficulty in getting on top of things. She couldn't blame the children's interruptions for a lot of it, although having Charlie home sick for the past two days with yet another bout of tonsillitis hadn't helped. What she needed was another pair of hands and, failing that, a better system.

'Honey, I've got to dash but ring me if you change your mind. I can head back in an hour or so after I've done my errands,' her mum said.

She wouldn't change her mind, she already knew that. Besides, Ally's idea of an evening out would last into the early hours of the morning. Rosie couldn't have asked that of her mum even if she'd wanted to.

Besides, who could go out socialising when there was a mountain of washing to do and nothing to talk about? And right now, she decided as she waved goodbye to her mum, if she gave in to demands and let the twins watch their favourite DVD, she had a precious hour to tackle folding the laundry.

Well into the hour, she realised she'd thought about nothing except a certain doctor in boardshorts, her mind leaping from question to assumption to imagery, all focused on him. It was the longest stretch of worry-free time she'd had since moving to Sydney from Canberra.

None of which left her any wiser about what she really wanted to know: would she see him again?

Or had walking away been the biggest mistake made by any single girl in Sydney this weekend?

On Tuesday morning, Rosie dropped Lucy at the school gate with ten minutes to spare and treated herself to a mental *Woohoo!* It felt like a major achievement and gave her a spark of hope that her attempts over the last few days to start developing a better time-management system were paying off. She watched as Lucy waited for a friend then gave one final wave to Rosie before she disappeared through the school gate, chatting happily.

She checked Charlie still had his seat belt on before pulling into the traffic.

'Do you think we'll make it in time?' she asked. Charlie's specialist appointment was in half an hour and, even though the clinic was in Bondi, Sydney traffic wasn't the best at this time of the day.

In the mirror she watched as Charlie shrugged his shoulders. 'Dr Masters will still see me if we're late, he'll probably be running behind anyway,' he told her.

He had a point, but she didn't want to arrive late, particularly when the specialist was fitting Charlie in as a favour. 'Have you thought some more about having your tonsils out? Dr Masters might suggest it today.'

'I don't want them out.'

Ah, so he hadn't budged. With Charlie's history of recurrent tonsillitis, it was only a matter of time before his tonsils had to come out. She was convinced these infections were exacerbating his other speech problems.

'There'd be no more sore throats, and you wouldn't have to miss so many Nippers' trainings.' Junior surf-lifesaving was one activity Charlie loved. She suppressed a twinge of guilt that she was using it to convince him to have the operation. 'Remember, I had my tonsils out when I was your age and I can still remember how much better I felt afterwards.'

'Yeah, but I don't like jelly.'

'What do you mean?' She glanced in the rear-view mirror to see Charlie pull a face.

'You told me you had jelly and ice cream in hospital. I don't like jelly.'

Who would have known jelly and ice cream would be a deal-breaker, not a deal-sweetener? 'They won't force you to eat jelly. Let's see what Dr. Masters has to say,' Rosie said as she pulled into the clinic car park, hoping she'd solved the jelly objection. What would he think of next?

The specialist suites were part of the Bondi Paediatric Medical Centre, a clinic Rosie had heard of but never visited. Charlie had been here before, but that had been with his parents. She pressed the button for the lift and looked around the ultra-modern foyer. There was a café on one side of the lifts and a pharmacy on the other. The building itself looked new, and the foyer and café were both brightly decorated in primary colours. Signs pointing down a corridor indicated directions to Physiotherapy and a hydrotherapy pool. The tenant directory beside the lift listed Speech Therapy, Occupational Therapy, General Practitioners and Psychology. There was a constant stream of families through the door.

Rosie and Charlie squeezed into the lift with a dozen other people and popped out at the third floor in front of the reception desk for the specialist suites. The girl directed them to the waiting room at the eastern end of the building and Rosie wasn't surprised to find the area had a magnificent view over the famous beach. Charlie immediately made himself comfortable in a bean-bag chair positioned in front of the enormous glass windows and settled down to watch the weekday surfers carving up the water.

Rosie flicked through a pile of magazines, all current issues, but the lure of the morning sunshine bouncing off the water was too enticing and she gave up on the magazines, instead choosing a chair where she could watch the beach too.

Movement to her left caught her attention and she turned to see a family coming through a doorway. The mother and daughter didn't hold her attention but the man behind them was a different story.

Nick.

The attraction she'd felt on Sunday had been strong, so strong she'd let her imagination run off in all sorts of directions. She'd entertained the possibility he'd be married with children but, still, her disappointment when she saw him with a family of his own surprised her.

From the safety of the anonymity of a crowded waiting room she let her gaze linger. There was no harm in looking. Or, at least, no harm in looking if no one knew.

Nick was dressed far more smartly than the other day but looked just as handsome. His dark grey trousers with a fine pinstripe and a crisp white cotton shirt looked simple but expensive. Quality. Style. The sleeves were rolled up to his elbows and his forearms and face were tanned golden brown. She sighed, daydreams of time with Nick fading into nothingness in view of the woman at his side.

He came to a stop just past the doorway and the woman and child continued on, saying thanks. He looked around the waiting room and at that moment Rosie realised he wasn't part of the family. This was his workplace. Visions of going with him, wherever he wanted, surged through her mind again. It was madness. Wholesale craziness. She knew that.

But it was a madness that left her tingling in such a delicious way it left her in no doubt that guardian aunt was not the only side of her still alive and kicking. She was still a woman, with desires and wants and needs, even if they had almost no chance of being satisfied in the near future. It was nice, though, very nice, to be reassured she hadn't totally disappeared, as a woman, during the events of the last months.

As he scanned the room, his gaze locked with hers and he lifted a hand in greeting as he broke into a broad smile, his cupid's-bow lips opening to reveal a set of perfect white teeth. Her response was automatic, the rush of warmth spreading upwards from deep in her belly until it gave her away with the blush that stole over her cheeks. She smiled through her embarrassment, still looking into blue-grey eyes that sparkled their pleasure at seeing her. All up, the exchange was only seconds. Certainly no one around them had noticed anything odd. People had their heads down in magazines, were murmuring to one another or were distracted by the demands of their children. For Rosie, though, it could have been minutes, hours even, that they'd looked at one another across the waiting room.

And Nick?

Nick had obviously remembered he was there to work and had broken the gaze after one more nod of his head and was scanning the waiting room. 'Charlie Jefferson?' Nick spoke softly but his deep voice penetrated through the general noise of a dozen waiting room conversations.

Rosie's eyes widened in surprise.

Nick wasn't just any doctor.

He was Dr Masters, Charlie's specialist.

Charlie appeared from his hiding place in the depths of the bean-bag where Nick hadn't had a hope of seeing him, and stood up at the sound of his name. Grabbing Rosie's hand, he tugged her to her feet. The pressure of his grip was enough to snap her into action and she followed Charlie as he crossed the waiting room.

'Hi, there, Charlie, nice to see you again.' He greeted Charlie first and the little boy smiled shyly at him, which was something, but, as expected, didn't speak. 'Rosie!' He held out a hand and shook hers briefly, his grip warm and sure, pleasure in his eyes. 'For a moment I thought you'd come to claim that cup of coffee I offered at the beach.'

Rosie saw Charlie look from her to Nick and back again, a frown creasing his forehead. He was still holding her hand and his fingers tightened on hers. She knew he was wondering how his aunt knew his specialist but his curiosity was not sufficient to get him asking questions.

'I didn't realise you were an ENT specialist,' she blurted out.

'We didn't have time for that conversation, it was a busy morning.' Nick's tone didn't change; he obviously didn't seem nonplussed as he led them along a short corridor, walking just in front since all three of them couldn't fit abreast and there was no way Charlie was letting go of his aunt. 'But, for me, things are now starting to fall into place. Lucy is Charlie's twin and you are their aunt. Yes?' He glanced back at her and she nodded in confirmation. 'Charlie's GP told me what happened.'

At her side, she felt Charlie relax a little, his fingers no longer clenched on her hand. Apparently he was satisfied that his aunt knowing his doctor was above-board. Perhaps he'd thought they'd been discussing him behind his back? Being talked about was something Charlie detested.

So at least there was now one less thing to explain in front of Charlie. He hadn't seen Dr Masters since before his parents had died and Rosie hadn't been keen on explaining the situation in front of her nephew.

Nick opened his office door, holding it open for them to enter. Rosie misjudged the width of the doorway and brushed against his arm as she passed him. Purely an accident, but the brief contact made her nerves jump to attention, covering her flesh in goose bumps. She hurriedly took one of the three seats alongside Nick's desk, leaving a chair for Charlie to sit next to her.

Nick settled himself into the third chair, sitting next to Charlie instead of behind his desk, surprising, but a nice touch.

'Not feeling too great, Charlie?' Nick asked. 'Doc Hawkins told me this is your second bout of tonsillitis since Christmas. Do you ever think of sharing it with your sister?'

Charlie smiled but shook his head.

'Let me have a look at this throat of yours, then.' He was natural with Charlie, focused on him, talking to him and not over his head, more adult-to-adult than adult-to-child. He was chalking up more points every second, with her at least, but she wasn't sure his warm demeanour was penetrating Charlie's armour.

'You know the drill.' Nick picked up his laryngoscope and Charlie dutifully opened his mouth.

'He's been on amoxicillin?' Nick asked Rosie. He glanced at her and another surge of attraction shot through her, so physical it was like a blow to the chest, and she literally had to catch her breath. He didn't seem at all distracted by her, whereas it was all she could do to concentrate on why they were there or even breathe normally.

'Yes.' She shifted her focus to Charlie as Nick had done and steadied her breathing before continuing. 'It helps but the episodes are so frequent and I'm concerned about Charlie missing so much school.' She caught Nick's eye, sending a silent message along with her words.

Nick's gaze narrowed slightly and he nodded, letting Rosie know he understood her meaning. 'Charlie, I'm almost out of tongue depressors.' Nick held up one of the flat wooden sticks he used. 'If I ring the girls at the front desk and ask for more, I bet you could fetch them for me quicker than I could. What do you think?' Charlie nodded and Nick dialled the reception desk, making his request and adding a suggestion that Charlie be allowed to choose a handful of sweets from the reception lolly jar, presumably a regular way of buying a few minutes with the child patient out of earshot. He turned back to Charlie. 'Thanks, mate, see you in a bit. And here's a tip—my receptionist never notices anyone hiding sweets in their pocket.' He winked at the little boy, whose eyes had grown wide. 'I do it all the time.'

The moment Charlie left the room Nick's focus turned to Rosie. His blue-grey eyes held her gaze and she fought the blush she was sure was sneaking its way up on her. This morning had confirmed her realisation on the beach: falling apart at the seams because of a good-looking guy was a sign she'd been more affected than she'd thought by the sudden change in her life. Too much time immersed in a world of school runs, packed lunches and mounds of washing must do things to a girl's brain!

'You're concerned about the amount of school Charlie's missing?'

Dismissing thoughts of how her insides were in danger of melting under his scrutiny, Rosie found her voice and got a grip. 'I'm not worried about it from an academic point of view but Charlie struggles socially at the best of times—'

'And missing school makes him feel more out of the loop,' said Nick, finishing off her sentence and her insides at the same time. A man who genuinely listened was one of her major weaknesses. Or so she'd just discovered. He'd turned his head slightly and was looking down at his desk to his left, deep in thought. Rosie was left to marvel that with this new revelation of his character, when added to his warmth, good looks and fabulous build, she hadn't simply melted into a pool of shiny warm jelly on the floor.

Maybe this vulnerability to a man who genuinely listened was so obvious only by its comparison to her recently ended relationship with Philip. Listening and Philip did not go together. Except for those with money and position. When those twin pillars of Philip's belief system talked, Philip most definitely listened. Nick, whom she'd probably now spent less than thirty minutes with in total, had probably listened to her more than Philip had in their entire relationship.

'I take it his selective mutism hasn't improved?'

Rosie shook her head. 'No, in fact, since he was diagnosed when he was four, he hasn't widened the circle of people he'll talk to. Not that anyone really expects him to at the moment, given the circumstances. But since his parents died there are now two fewer people whom he *will* talk to.'

'How many in total will he talk to?'

'Five. My parents, his twin, me and his best friend from kindy, who is now at school with him.'

'He makes eye contact with me. Does he do that with other people too?'

Rosie nodded. 'For the most part, once he's familiar with someone. But he just won't, or literally can't, talk to people. He freezes.'

'Eye contact is a start but it's not very encouraging if he's not making any other progress.' Nick paused briefly. 'Do you think these frequent bouts of tonsillitis are genuine? Remember, he's seen his GP, not me, for some of them. You think he's happy enough about going to school?' His head was cocked to one side, waiting for her input.

'I've only been caring for the twins for two months but he's had two episodes of tonsillitis in that time, three since last December, and, in my opinion, they've all been the real deal.'

'Do you think the death of his parents has contributed at all?'

'Do I think there's a psychological aspect to it? Like his selective mutism?'

Nick nodded.

'There could be, it's hard to know for sure, although his psychologist thinks he's coping pretty well.' Rosie found by pretending she was talking to Charlie's GP, not Nick, she could talk almost naturally. 'But that's another reason I don't want his routine to change too much. I'm worried his mutism might get worse if he's regularly away from school because of tonsillitis.'

'So the tonsillectomy would mean a few more days off school but you think he'd benefit in the long run.' Again, he'd neatly summarised her thoughts.

'Yes. His psychologist agrees too, obviously on the basis that you consider it necessary.'

'Looking at his tonsils today I think it's reasonable to take them out, both from a medical and social point of view.'

Charlie reappeared, sucking with concentration, a fresh supply of tongue depressors in his right hand and his left hand holding his bulging pants pocket shut.

'Fantastic. Thanks, Charlie.' Nick took the handful from Charlie, pointedly ignoring his overflowing pocket. 'Have a seat, there's something I need to discuss with you.' Rosie swallowed a laugh as Charlie slid awkwardly into his seat, clearly not wanting to risk a single lolly spilling out. 'Your tonsils are pretty inflamed, all red and swollen. Your throat must be pretty sore and I'm guessing it's pretty hard to talk to Rosie, even without a lolly in your mouth. Is that right?'

Charlie nodded and quickly popped another lolly, red-and-green striped, into his mouth.

'They're my favourite, you know. You've got good taste,' Nick added, nodding at Charlie's mouth before continuing as if he hadn't changed the subject. Charlie's eyes grew wide at the comment and he looked pleased with Nick's attention. Rosie crossed her fingers and hoped that Nick's rapport with Charlie would get her nephew thinking differently about the operation. 'If I take your tonsils out, it'll be sore for a few days, but not much worse than you feel when you have tonsillitis. You might still get a cold now and again but you won't get the same sore throats any more. Does that sound like a good idea?'

Charlie looked at Rosie and she knew what he was thinking.

'He won't have to eat jelly, will he? I had to eat jelly when I had my tonsils out and Charlie doesn't like it.'

'Well, when Rosie was little, back in the olden days...'

Nick winked at Charlie '…the nurses were very strict and everyone had to eat jelly, but now, if I tell the nurses no jelly, that's all there is to it.'

Rosie could well imagine. She didn't think there'd be too many complaints no matter what Nick asked the nursing staff.

'Do we have a deal?'

Charlie glanced at Rosie then back to Nick, looking at him for a few seconds before nodding solemnly. Nick kept a solemn face, too, holding out a hand, and Charlie took it, shaking on their deal, all the while sucking on the lolly determinedly. Charlie was nothing if not determined. In everything he did, including not talking. It made it all the more amazing that Nick had managed to convince Charlie to have the surgery.

'I'll look at my operating schedule and work out when I can fit Charlie in. I'll ring you and let you know what we can arrange. But whenever it is, there will definitely be no jelly coming anywhere near you, young man, doctor's orders.'

Charlie beamed at Nick and didn't pull away when Nick placed a hand on his shoulder as he walked them out. They were in the hallway when Charlie turned and ran back into Nick's office, leaving Rosie staring blankly after her nephew, his behaviour out of character. 'Maybe he forgot something?' They didn't have time to wonder, though, as Charlie was already tearing back to them, a secret smile dancing around the corners of his mouth.

It was much the same way Rosie felt, too, as she waved goodbye to Nick in the waiting room. Because, whatever else happened, she was at least guaranteed to speak to Nick again soon.

Nick stopped by the receptionist desk to see who his next patient was, suppressing mild irritation when he was told they hadn't shown up, with no phone call of explanation.

'It'll give you a chance to look at these.' She handed over a thick yellow envelope marked 'Confidential'.

Nick cocked an eyebrow, asking, 'The revised partnership agreement?'

She nodded. 'I'll hold your calls for half an hour so you can go through it.' She picked up another bundle of papers and slid it into his hands on top of the first envelope. 'And if you get time, these referrals and reports need to be done. Sooner. Not later.'

'You're a slave-driver, you're meant to protect me from the world, not be the one who attacks me,' muttered Nick, but it was good-natured and even managed to bring out a glimmer of a smile to soften his receptionist's serious features. He tucked the pile of papers under his arm and headed back to his office, free to contemplate the fact that a missed appointment wasn't what was irritating him, and the partnership papers weren't what was uppermost in his mind. It was the fact that he could've kept talking with Rosie and Charlie if his next appointment hadn't been looming.

Charlie was intriguing and he was determined to get him to talk at some stage. And his aunt? She fell into the intriguing category, too, a category that had been dismally empty for some considerable time now. Together, they made an interesting pair.

Once at his desk, he slapped the pile of papers down, resolved to comb through the final agreement he'd been impatient to receive. Then his eyes caught a bright colour and his papers lay forgotten.

A boiled lolly, red-and-green striped, shiny and hard, lay where it had been placed carefully in the centre of his notepad. He picked it up, inspected it momentarily and then lifted the pad on which someone had written, 'They're my favourite, too.'

'Bingo,' muttered Nick as he popped the lolly into his mouth. 'He's talking to me.'

Rosie had long since tucked Charlie and Lucy into bed and they were now fast asleep. In the last two months, this had become the time of the day she most needed. It was also the time she most dreaded. She needed the breathing space but being alone left her facing the fact she was also lonely. Dreadfully so.

Tonight, though, there was a certain comfort in being lonely. For a start, it made sense of her reaction to Nick today—and the first time she'd met him, too, if she was honest. If she wasn't so lonely, if her life hadn't changed so radically overnight with the unexpected deaths of her brother and sister-in-law, she wouldn't be acting so out of character. She wouldn't be knocked sideways by a stranger with a kind smile. All right, a killer smile. She'd noticed him, she was no nun, but she wouldn't normally be rendered speechless or breathless or experiencing any of the symptoms he induced in her. That was obviously due to the demands of her new life. And her grief.

She and the children had encased themselves in a bubble. Insular was the word for it. She saw her parents but they understood the circumstances all too well since they shared the same loss.

Thanks to Nick, she could now say some feeling had returned and it was good. Noticing a very attractive man was a pleasant way of being enticed back into the land of the living but it didn't mean anything more than that. She was only *really* noticing him because of her loneliness. It didn't mean what she was trying to achieve for the twins was under threat.

Her sole focus was to give her niece and nephew a sense of normality, knowing her own needs could wait. She was the adult. Her reaction to Nick had reminded her she was well and truly alive and although her needs might need to wait, they hadn't been obliterated. She toyed momentarily with the idea of socialising beyond her immediate family so her old self didn't disappear totally. The thought didn't appeal, not yet.

And yet the reality was she was sitting on the couch, alone, at eight o'clock at night, empty hours stretching before her. And that reality didn't appeal either. In her old life she would have been heading out to watch a movie with a girlfriend or more likely to dinner with Philip and his political cronies. Now she was sitting on the couch contemplating making lunches and folding washing. Deciding she was too tired to do any of that, she flicked through the CD collection, looking for a way to break the silence. But the CDs belonged to her brother, David, and his wife, Anna. She didn't want that reminder tonight.

Most of her possessions were still in Canberra. She'd jumped on a plane when her parents had called her after the accident and had only been back briefly once. She had meant to have her things sent to her but somehow there was always something else needing to be done first. Now was as good a time as any to let her ex know her plans. Apart from a few clothes, the rest of her things were still in the apartment they'd shared.

She picked up her mobile and hit the automatic dial for Philip's mobile phone.

'Rosie!' He knew it was her before she spoke. There was some comfort in knowing he hadn't deleted her number from his phone memory. Yet. 'How are you?'

How should she respond? She knew Philip wouldn't want to hear the truth. She'd spent the past week looking after one sick child while trying to make sure the other got enough attention too and making sure the wheels didn't fall off their lives completely. She'd learnt long ago that Philip was one of those people for whom 'How are you?' was really a rhetorical question. So she gave her standard response.

'Good. Have you got a minute? I need to sort out getting some of my things sent up.'

'I'm on my way out, we'll talk about it on Saturday when I get to Sydney. For the dinner.' He paused and she could hear in his voice that he was frowning, displeased. 'With the New Zealand Prime Minister. You did remember?'

'Yes,' Rosie fibbed. He'd been right to doubt her, she'd

totally forgotten. Her life was very much lived from one day to the next at the moment and Saturday night was still four days away. She wanted to go to a formal political event even less than she wanted to spend every night at home for the next year, but she'd promised. Had she just forgotten or had she just hoped the function would go away if she ignored it?

'Are you sure—?'

Philip read her intentions before she'd fully realised herself what she'd been about to say. 'You promised, Rosie, and yes, it is important you're seen with me.'

Important she was seen with him, not important that she *be* with him. There was a difference. And it rankled.

'I'm flying in at six and the car will come straight from the airport to pick you up. Formal dress.'

What was the point in refusing? He was right, she *had* promised, and Rosie didn't break promises or let people down, even if they were ex-boyfriends. There were lots of things Rosie didn't do. But one thing she said a lot was, 'Sure.' Sure, no problem; sure, it'll put me out but don't you worry; sure, sure, sure. She sure was sick of saying 'sure'.

'We'll talk then. Bye.'

Typically, Philip had turned the conversation to his needs. He hadn't even offered to bring any of her things with him. He could easily have thrown some stuff in a suitcase. Members of Parliament didn't seem to have the same luggage restrictions as mere mortals. All her evening dresses were in Canberra, he could easily have brought something for her to wear. Rosie debated whether to call him back and then decided it would be easier to buy something new. Easier for her—or easier for him?

He'd do it if she asked directly, she had to give him that, but maybe only because it affected him directly? He wouldn't want to turn up and have her unable to go for lack of something to wear. But for the same reason he couldn't be counted on to bring the dress and shoes she actually requested. He'd bring what he deemed suitable. It was unlikely to be the same thing.

She tossed the phone on the couch beside her and closed her eyes. Perhaps if she shut everything out for a few moments she'd find the energy to get up and finish the day's chores.

Seconds after she'd thrown the phone down it rang, startling her. Philip ringing to see what he could bring? She may as well glance out the window and check if the pigs were flying.

'Hello?'

'Hi, Rosie? It's Nick Masters.'

A warm glow spread through her, replacing the low feeling she'd been grappling with even before she had called Philip. 'Nick, hi.'

'I've just checked my operating schedule for the next fortnight. I know it's late, but I'm only just out of surgery and I got the feeling you're an information person like me so you'd rather know sooner than later.'

Rosie managed 'Thanks' in reply, stunned he could know that about her in such a short space of time. Or at all. Would any of her past boyfriends have had such an insight into her character?

'I can fit Charlie in on Monday week. I operate at St Catherine's that day so it's close for you.'

'Monday's good. St Catherine's good.' Some proper sentences would also be good, she muttered mentally. Come on, get it together. The guy doesn't know you're a house-bound loony, don't let the secret out now! She kick-started her brain into gear. 'Great. And you're right, I do like to get all the facts, then I can deal with it, plan, work out what I'm going to do.' So far so good. 'Things are much less stressful when the information is on the table and you're not left second-guessing. Not that I was scared about you operating…' She stumbled to an embarrassed silence.

Nick didn't miss a beat, simply laughing as if she'd been joking. 'I'm glad to hear it, although most people are terrified, some not so secretly, at the thought of their child having surgery. I'll get the forms posted to you but he'll need to be admitted at seven a.m. Can you manage that?'

It would mean juggling Lucy's schedule but that wasn't Nick's problem. 'Yes, I'll sort something out.'

'What about your work, can you take time off?'

'I'm on a leave of absence from my job to concentrate on the children.'

There was a brief silence at the other end. Had she scared him off with too much information? 'Maybe once I get Charlie sorted for you, that will help things settle down.' She got the feeling it wasn't what he wanted to say, or ask, but that's all it was. A feeling. And she didn't know him well enough to ask.

'I hope so. It might be a start at least.'

'Let me know if there's anything I can do,' he offered.

'Thanks, Nick, but I doubt you have time to worry about how your patients are going to organise their lives.' She settled back against the deep cushions of the couch, conscious she was behaving as if she was readying herself for a nice long chat with a good friend.

'Not usually. But most of my private patients have a partner or, to be honest, a nanny to help pick up the slack, and in the public hospitals there's Family and Community Services help if necessary. It's no difficulty to schedule things to suit you, you just need to say.'

'I appreciate that, but we'll be fine, this time at least. We'll see you on the sixteenth, and thank you.' She hesitated, unused to the feeling of having help offered, of accepting it, then added, 'If I get stuck and need an appointment changed, I'll remember your invitation. It's very kind of you.'

He said goodbye and she ended the call, wondering what he'd wanted to say or ask when she'd mentioned her work leave. She shrugged, knowing she'd never know and it probably didn't matter. It was just one more sign of how insular she'd become, that she could sit analysing the things an almost-stranger hadn't said during a routine phone call.

On another note, a more positive note, the phone call had helped her more than Nick would know. To be asked how she was coping, whether something would suit *her*, made all the difference. She suspected she wasn't coping all that well given her growing preoccupation with her nephew's specialist, a man who'd rung only to schedule surgery. A man unlikely to have any interest in an overwhelmed, grieving aunt. But if she allowed herself to ignore those obvious objections, he'd still managed to make her feel she was cared about. He'd managed to make her feel less alone at precisely the time she'd needed that reassurance, however fleeting it might be.

The contrast between that phone call and the earlier one with Philip was marked. Philip, who should have asked after the children, out of politeness if not out of a sense of concern, hadn't, yet a virtual stranger had.

Returning to Canberra to live with the children was one of the options she was thinking over. After her phone call with her ex, that option was looking bleaker. What was there for her, for any of them, if her breakup with Philip was going to be permanent?

Or perhaps, she reflected, recalling how her tongue had frozen and her belly had sprung to life at the sight of Nick today, what had there ever been there for her? Even *with* Philip?

CHAPTER THREE

NICK retied his black bow-tie, struggling to get it sitting properly but unable to give it the concentration it needed. His work schedule and goals were up in lights in his head, distracting him from the immediate task at hand. He had, just yesterday, signed the final partnership papers. He was now a full partner in the medical clinic. He was finally scaling the mountain of goals he'd been working towards. Buying into the practice meant a significant amount of debt but it was debt necessary to building a business, unlike the mound of debt he'd only finally cleared these last months. That had been a noose around his neck, nothing but a dead weight.

Now he'd shrugged it off and had embarked on this new, productive phase of his life. His work was building up, referrals were coming in apace. He felt more confident than he'd felt in years.

He pulled on the ends of his tie one final time, shrugging at his reflection in the mirror. His tie looked like it was supposed to. Close enough, anyway. It was just a tie. He ran his fingers through his hair. He'd long since given up on trying to get it to sit neatly, his cowlick making that impossible. He was only aiming for semi-presentable. Ditto for the bow-tie.

Grabbing his dinner jacket as he headed out the door, he knew he was looking forward to the evening. He'd stopped the downward spiral that had been his life for the past few years.

He was a successful medical specialist with a growing practice. Not a man with a failed marriage and a huge, useless debt. His single-minded pursuit of stability was at last paying off.

He slung his jacket in the back of his car and allowed himself a wry grin as he slid behind the wheel of his old Holden wagon, proof positive that he wasn't completely out of the hole his ex-wife had dug for him. It was a sure-fire bet no one else would be heading for the Opera House tonight in anything as old as this but his finances didn't stretch to splurging on a new vehicle. This one did the job.

He was used to making do.

Sometimes it seemed that was all he'd done for years.

Make do. Make do while he worked and strove single-mindedly to fulfil the goals he'd been set on since late adolescence. Stability. Security. Respectability.

And, after a string of major setbacks, it was finally all in his sights.

So tonight, to celebrate, he would mingle and dance and enjoy the kudos that came with being a medical specialist, the newest partner in a successful practice.

Rosie opened the door to find Philip himself on the front step, immaculate as always. As usual he looked made for his suit, probably because his suit had been made for him and he wore it as if he deserved it.

He leant forward and Rosie hesitated. Cheek? Lips? Handshake? What was the etiquette the first time you saw your ex after you'd separated? Philip clearly thought lips were in order but she found herself offering her cheek for a kiss. The first time she'd consciously gone against what Philip wanted? Correction. The second. Taking up the guardianship of the twins and leaving Canberra had definitely *not* been what Philip had wanted.

But was that really because he cared for Rosie enough to

spend his life with her? She knew it wasn't enough for her; if it had been she wouldn't have called it off because she was moving. For the same reasons, she knew it was the same for him. If he'd cared so much about her, he would've tried to make a long-distance relationship work. After all, she was still contemplating a return to Canberra. So she knew his chagrin was more because she had disturbed the convenient, established order of their lives together than because he was heartbroken.

'Hi. Did you have a good trip?'

He nodded. 'You look nice, you don't wear much yellow. It suits you.' He glanced at the dress again, frowning slightly as he took in the drape of the fabric, which left nothing to the imagination. Yet, except for her shoulders and arms, and a rather revealing cleavage, she was fully covered and the dress wasn't too tight, just sculpted as if made for her. 'I grabbed it yesterday from the remnants of the end-of-summer sales.' She resisted tugging at the low neckline. If she was going to wear it, she may as well act comfortable in it. But she hadn't been joking when she'd said it was from the remnants—it had been the only decent thing left that both fitted her and had been in her price bracket. 'Why don't you come in and say hello to the kids and my mum?'

Philip checked his watch. He was looking for an excuse, she knew, and was waiting for her to let him off the hook. Fair enough, she had to admit she normally would have done so, but tonight a small, unfamiliar feeling of defiance was niggling her. She was already doing him a favour by going to the dinner. For once, he could do something for her. He hadn't even offered to bring any of her things up from Canberra. She laughed at herself for letting that gripe surface again. 'I need to grab my bag anyway,' she said as she stepped back and headed down the hall, not particularly caring whether he followed.

It only took minutes to wish he hadn't. Lucy, Charlie and

Rosie's mum were in the family room, Rosie's mum and Philip were making stilted conversation and Lucy was being her normal extroverted self, forcing Philip to pay her some awkward attention. As for Charlie, Philip ignored the little boy who had never spoken to him despite having met him a number of times during Rosie and Philip's trips up to Sydney. Philip, silver-tongued with statesmen, was as tongue-tied and awkward with Charlie as Charlie was mute with most of the world. Until tonight Rosie had excused her partner but that irritated feeling wasn't abating. Couldn't a grown man think of something to say to a little boy that only required a shake or nod of the head in response?

After a couple of minutes Rosie had had enough. Picking up her bag and kissing them all goodnight, she took Philip away, ending everyone's discomfort. It was more confirmation that she'd been right not to move the children to Canberra.

At least, not right away.

Conversation was one-sided on the drive to the Opera House. The glass screen between the chauffeur and their seats was up and in the privacy of the back Philip delivered his thoughts as to who he would introduce her to, who he wanted her to chat to and for how long. Rosie closed her eyes momentarily and Philip laid a hand on her arm, apparently reading her thoughts, saying, 'I know these things can be tiresome.' Which Rosie knew he didn't think at all so he must mean tiresome for her. 'But you've always handled yourself so well.'

'Philip, I promised you I'd come tonight and I'll do the right thing, and I'll do it all with my most charming smile.' She meant it too, although it would come at some effort. The couch she'd been lamenting four days ago now seemed much the preferable option.

'Any more thought about moving home?'

'I don't know what I'm going to do, the children can't be moved right now.'

Philip sighed, drumming his fingers on his lap. 'Rosie, you don't look yourself, you look exhausted. And you must be missing work. Besides, you only took a leave of absence, you're going to have to decide what to do soon.'

She wanted to argue but she gave it up and slumped a little. He was right. About some things. 'I agree it's been hard making the adjustment but that doesn't mean it's the wrong thing to do. I'm where I need to be and where I want to be. I miss work, true, but I'll get back to it in time, just not right now. I also agree I'm tired and if I'm not glowing with happiness, it's because I'm grieving for my brother and his wife. Those are consequences I have to deal with. It doesn't translate into me wanting to ditch the children.'

'You seemed to ditch Canberra easily enough.' Rosie flinched at the hurt in his voice. He'd done his best not to show she'd hurt him before she'd gone, but she'd known it was his pride behind that because she'd left him feeling rejected.

'I didn't end things with you easily. Honestly, it makes me sad, but now I've had time apart to think, I'm pretty sure we'd run our course. I said it was better to call it off because I didn't want to be making promises I couldn't keep. And I think I was right.' She was distracted for a moment as she saw they'd arrived at the Opera House and had pulled into the queue of chauffeur-driven cars which, one by one, were depositing their passengers at the foot of the red-carpeted stairs up to the white-sailed building. 'And you were also clear you couldn't move with me. So there was no other reasonable alternative.'

He didn't answer her, just gave a sharp nod of the head. It was her turn to lay a hand on his arm, stroking the expensive fabric of his suit jacket lightly. 'I know you're hurt that I left, but in the interests of us salvaging our friendship, can you accept this is what I had to do?'

'I'm no good with children.' Was he explaining why he

hadn't been able to consider moving with her? Or attempting a long-distance relationship? It sounded like an explanation. Perhaps it was?

'I'm not asking you to be.' Not strictly true, she'd deliberately tested him tonight when she'd invited him in and he'd struggled. 'But that's what my life is now. Quite frankly, I don't know what shape things are going to take, but the children will be a central part no matter what.'

The car was pulling up in front of the steps, the door was opened for them and Philip emerged first, waiting to help Rosie out of the car. He might be cross with her, because she'd let him down and hurt him, but with Philip that would be no reason not to keep up appearances. How had he explained her absence so far from any number of functions in Canberra? After being an established couple over the last couple of years, did anyone even know they were separated?

Rosie allowed him to escort her into the function room. Philip kept her close and Rosie knew why. He liked to make an entrance and they made a striking couple: she was five foot ten in bare feet and Philip was several inches taller, so their height alone made people notice them. In politics, being noticed was part of the game if you wanted to climb to the top.

Rosie knew she was an asset in this regard. She'd never minded, it was the way the world worked, but now she questioned that assumption—had she just begun thinking like that because she'd been so fully immersed in that world? Maybe the rest of the world didn't function so superficially?

She scanned the already crowded room and realised it wasn't fair, not entirely. There were plenty of familiar faces and among them were some people she'd always enjoyed seeing, it wasn't all rubbing shoulders for the sake of it. Tonight, though, pleasant people or not, it wasn't where she wanted to be. She'd promised Philip she'd mingle cheerfully, but for the life of her she couldn't imagine having anything of interest to contribute. When had she last managed to read the weekend papers when the news wasn't already three days old?

For now, though, she waited dutifully next to Philip in the line to meet the Australian Prime Minister and his New Zealand counterpart. Rosie towered over the Australian PM but, then, so did most people. He remembered meeting her before, a fact which clearly pleased Philip. Maybe this would give her some bonus points and allow her to sneak off from her 'official' duties a bit earlier.

Philip introduced her to the minister for education and his wife before excusing himself. The minister was a rather dull man, his wife even more so, and she knew she'd been delivered to them to pay Philip's dues without him having to endure them. After a few minutes she made her own excuses and made her way to the minister for health, collecting a glass of white wine along the way. The health minister was also someone Philip wanted her to talk to but at least he was interesting. He'd been a doctor in his pre-government life so they'd be able to find some common ground.

She was here.

Nick had noticed her the moment she'd entered the room. In a room filled wall to wall with ageing men in black suits and women wearing predominantly safe little black dresses, Rosie shone like a star in her canary-yellow dress.

Her shoulder-length sandy-blonde hair had been pinned back from her face and with her summer tan she looked beautiful, but he was sure he could still see the traces of shadows around her eyes, the faint tinge of tiredness he'd seen at the beach and his office. Even so, and even competing with the stunning backdrop of the lights of Sydney Harbour, she had no trouble capturing his attention.

He mingled, all the time aware of where she was. She'd made an entrance on the arm of a similarly noticeable man—

taller, younger and better-looking than many of the other men in the room. The guy didn't fit the picture he realised he'd built up around Rosie, of a young woman on her own, managing a difficult set of circumstances. Had he got her wrong?

Right now Rosie was talking to the minister for health. Nick couldn't see the guy who had accompanied Rosie into the function but he didn't waste time trying to find him either. One man's loss. Was what? His ticket to making this evening the celebration he'd been planning?

The instant attraction he'd felt for her, stirred by her combination of vitality and vulnerability, was showing no signs of lessening tonight. Not a chance of it with her wearing a dress that looked like it was poured over her skin. He'd given himself permission to relax and enjoy the evening. He didn't have to get involved, he was allowed to have fun and if he could have fun with Rosie—well, that was even better.

He ignored the nagging suspicion in the back of his mind that he was flirting with danger by spending time with her. She didn't strike him as the type who went for brief dalliances— neither was he, for that matter—but this pull between them was there and the question had to be asked. If Rosie needed a night off from her responsibilities this could work out perfectly for both of them.

He cut across the room as she left the minister's side, walking swiftly so he could catch her before she began another conversation.

Rosie excused herself from the health minister as another couple approached him, congratulating herself for getting off to a good start. 'That's two prime ministers and two ministers down in the first half-hour,' she muttered as she weaved through the crowded room, 'and I think I can count the minister for education as two ministers since he was hard enough work. Time for a break before dinner.' She'd walk the room, nodding and smiling and looking like she had somewhere to go so no one stopped her to chat.

Not more than half a dozen steps later someone said her name behind her. So much for her plan.

'Rosie Jefferson, what a happy coincidence.'

She turned, her smile immediate when she saw who it was. 'Nick!' And just like that, the head-spinning tingles were back, along with the desire to step into his arms and go with him. Madness! With an effort, she said, 'What on earth are you doing here?'

'You don't think a simple doctor is worthy of such high-flying company?' His grin was magic as he gestured to take in the room full of politicians and other movers and shakers. Philip looked good in his dinner suit but on Nick it was elevated to a whole new level of deliciousness. His broad, straight shoulders perfectly suited to jackets, he could have stepped off a catwalk. And she knew in an instant Nick hadn't spent nearly the same sum on his suit—another end-of-summer remnant?

'Maybe not a question of being worthy, but is this really your usual Saturday night entertainment?' She was fishing, shamelessly so, and she didn't care. She needed to know whatever she could about him. How he cut his toast, where his favourite beach was, whether he had struggled to tie his bow-tie tonight…how he'd react if she reached out now and tugged on it, loosened it… She widened her eyes at the thought and swallowed. Hard. Stuttering, she tried to cover the fact her mind had wandered off into fantasy territory. Again. 'I wouldn't have pictured you here.'

'It shows?' He looked crestfallen but was clearly anything but. 'You're right, I'm an impostor. I only scored an invite as a token Kiwi since the PM's in town. I was one of the best they could scrounge up, the rest are working in bars and chasing the surf. But, still, what gave me away?'

'Your dinner suit looks as new as my dress.'

He made a great show of slowly examining her dress, managing not to focus on her cleavage. Full points there, but she was left tingling under his scrutiny, feeling all too revealed. She hadn't enjoyed anything as much in a long, long time. She *really* had to get out more.

'The suit's brand-new, the old one's in New Zealand and hasn't been worn for the best part of a decade. As for your dress, you didn't need to tell me it was new.' He glanced over her shoulder. 'You left the tag on.'

Horrified, she tried to both look and feel over her shoulder, while he stood chuckling with what appeared to be great amusement. After some indiscreet attempts to feel the back of her dress for the price tag, the realisation dawned. 'There's no tag, right?'

'Right. I just wanted to check my hunch. But why the new dress? Is there someone you need to impress or do you crave new dresses like I crave Perky Nanas?'

'You crave happy grandmas?'

'Ah, that qualifies as yet another of my cross-cultural faux pas. Of course you don't have Perky Nanas in Australia.'

She shook her head. She really hoped he had a good explanation.

'They're a chocolate bar, chewy banana flavour.' He stuck his hands in his pockets and laughed out loud. 'Your expression just then was priceless. Horror to relief in one second flat. So, translation over, which is it? Out to impress or you have a fashion addiction?'

'Neither. All my gear's in Canberra.'

He looked blank. Her turn to tease, knowing full well he was drawing a blank on why her gear would be in Canberra, not what Canberra actually was. 'You know, the city purpose built for the politicians, the capital of Australia?'

'Sure, and also the logical place to keep your wardrobe when you live in Sydney.'

'There aren't so many moths down there.' She looked him dead in the eye. 'They don't like the cold.'

He raised an eyebrow, looked her dead in the eye back, his face serious, and said, 'I suspect you are playing with me now. Not nice when I'm a hapless immigrant. Isn't the new Government's immigration policy meant to be, shall we say, based on more tolerant ideals? Be nice to strangers, no teasing?'

She didn't miss a beat. 'There's an exemption clause for New Zealanders.'

His laughter rang clear and true. 'Touché. And as for Canberra, what's the story there?'

'I moved here for the twins.' She'd recovered her equilibrium and was discovering their verbal exchange was as exhilarating as her earlier fantasies about Nick and bow-ties. 'I haven't had a chance to go back and sort my things out yet.'

'Charlie's GP didn't mention that.'

'He probably didn't see it as relevant to Charlie's medical care.'

Again, she had the feeling he wanted to ask her more but he simply nodded before saying, 'So tell me how you scored an invitation tonight. You're not the PM's doctor or someone famous I should know, are you?'

She shook her head. 'I'm a GP but my ex-partner is in politics and I'd promised to come. So here I am. But how did you really get an invite? You can't tell me someone trawled the streets to scrounge up some reputable Kiwis.'

'I'm now considered a respectable, presentable ex-pat Kiwi, who can usually be relied on not to embarrass our small nation when out in public. I think that was the job description for this evening.' He paused for effect then gave her the real reason. 'And Tim, one of my best mates, is Harriet Carter's media advisor—that might have had something to do with it.'

'The New Zealand Prime Minister's media advisor? Your circle of friends is impressive.'

'Thereby making me impressive by association?'

'I guess it does.' From where she stood he was impressive all on his own. The way he wore his suit was just the start of a long list entitled 'Impressive Things About Nick'. The fullness of his lips, the way his hair fell from the cowlick at his forehead, his height, the colours of a changeable sea she now saw were intermingled in his irises, his warmth, his sense of humour, the fact he seemed kind.

The fact he was looking at her like she'd spaced out, which she had. 'I guess it does,' she repeated, for lack of something new to say.

'Good. Since it's settled I'm impressive, can I steal you away for a few minutes or do you have some more tiresome politicians you need to talk to?'

'Don't you?'

'Like I said, I'm a token for the evening. Consider me the equivalent of a designer-clad game-show hostess, here simply for looks. In my book, that means my only responsibility is to enjoy myself and I came prepared to do exactly that. My chances of that, I think, are greatly improved by your being here.'

He smiled at her as he finished talking, banishing Rosie's thoughts of any other people she was supposed to talk to. His smile was capable of making her forget her own name, let alone everything else going on around her. Besides, what was currently going on around her was easily forgotten.

'I'm sure politics can do without me, I'm all yours.'

Nick swapped her empty glass for a full one, taking a glass of water for himself before moving across to the expanse of floor-to-ceiling windows that overlooked Sydney Harbour.

The Harbour Bridge spanned the sea as the ferries criss-crossed below it, the old-fashioned green and gold wooden boats adding some character among the modern, high-speed white ferries. The lights of the houses on the north shore provided a glittering backdrop to the darkness of the ocean.

They stood side by side, looking out. 'Have you settled into Sydney okay?'

'I'm from here originally but I'm still finding my feet in the parenting department, so I don't think I've really registered where I am.' She was surprised to find herself being so frank with him; since her brother's death she'd been playing her cards close to her chest, not admitting much about her real feelings to anyone. She turned towards him, wondering how he'd take her admission she wasn't totally on top of things.

He held her gaze with his own. 'I'm not surprised. Your life's been tipped upside down and inside out. Do you know if you plan on staying here? Your gear is still in Canberra…' He let the question hang in the air between them, as if there was more riding on it than where her evening gowns happened to be hung.

'I moved here to look after Charlie and Lucy. I'm their legal guardian and I wasn't prepared to disrupt them any more than necessary by moving them to Canberra. Philip, my ex, couldn't leave Canberra so we decided it was easiest to call it quits.' Had he noticed she had avoided answering his question?

'Leaving you where, exactly?'

She didn't answer for a moment. Where did it leave her? 'If you want the honest truth, I don't know. I scarcely have time to work out what day it is at the moment let alone think about what *I* want, or need.'

'I can only imagine. I'm going to push my luck and ask another personal question I have no business asking. Blame it on my gaucheness as a foreigner.'

'Hmm,' she said, noncommittal but not at all put out.

'Why couldn't Philip commute if you wanted to be together? It's not uncommon for politicians.'

'Maybe not established ones but Philip is still junior and he has big ambitions. He wants a ministerial appointment, another reason why he won't budge from Canberra, and he knows he needs to impress the right people. Which is why I'm here tonight.'

'You want to impress the right people?' He was jesting but his smile had tightened.

Her denial was automatic. 'I'm here to help *him* impress people. I've been his partner for over two years, the change has been hard on him and I promised I'd support him tonight, so he wouldn't have to come stag or explain where I was.'

'He's lucky you're so understanding.'

'I feel bad, as I'm the one who left.'

'Do you do a lot of things because of guilt?'

'Pardon?'

'You are very kind, turning your life upside down for the twins and then feeling guilty about your ex when the circumstances were not under your control. I suspect only extreme kindness, selflessness even, would make someone in your current situation brave a night like tonight.' His words hung in the air between them like a physical caress. Then he winked and said, 'It was either that or the free drinks.'

She laughed, grateful he'd handed her an easy way out of having to respond to his observation. 'The free drinks get me every time.'

An announcement asking everyone to take their seats interrupted them but Nick added a quick final sentence as the crowd started moving towards the dining room. 'And dancing? How does dancing figure in your plans this evening? The music's free, my dance card is empty and the dance floor is stamped with your name.'

'Dancing sounds lovely.' Anything would sound lovely if proposed by Nick.

'Great.' Nick placed his hand on her elbow, turning her away from the windows and back towards the tables. The touch of his hand sent a bolt of electricity through her, igniting the warm glow and turning her insides into a liquid pool of desire. For a moment she stood as though bolted to the floor. It made no sense to be shocked by her reaction to him, she should be getting used to his effect on her by now. But each time was like the first time.

Could she really claim he only affected her like this because she'd been so isolated recently? Maybe dancing with him wasn't such a great idea after all. For him, it would be just a dance. For her, she was in danger of melting on the dance floor if she spent more than a few seconds held in his arms.

Her feet found the power of movement and she headed towards the dining area with him, his hand resting lightly on her back, her insides screaming every step of the way for more. More talking, more touches of his hand. More everything.

And she knew then that with him a dance could never be a dance.

Nothing could be ordinary with Dr Nick Masters.

But that's exactly where her life was and where she had to keep it: as ordinary as possible, for the sake of two very vulnerable children.

For once, Rosie was thrilled the dinner speeches went on ad nauseam since they made table conversation redundant.

Philip had asked her where she'd been and he'd been unhappy she'd spent a large proportion of the time during pre-dinner drinks talking to her nephew's specialist, whether or not he knew the New Zealand PM, an exaggeration Rosie had thrown in as a sweetener without intending to. Since when had she told white lies? She'd crossed her fingers hoping Philip never got the chance to ask Nick how that non-existent acquaintance had begun.

Philip had no claims on her but he might fairly ask her why she'd misled him. She didn't have the answer. Except she wasn't ready to explain Nick. Or, rather, to explain how she felt around Nick. That she was in the grip of an adolescent fantasy, one-sided, impossible. If she gave voice to it, she just knew it would vanish in a puff of smoke.

As the last speech ended, Rosie glanced over her shoulder and looked straight into Nick's appreciative eyes. He was seated a couple of tables away and he raised his glass ever so slightly in a discreet toast. He'd have had a good view of her bare back and semi-profile the entire evening. Had he been looking? As he lowered his glass and grinned, she knew he had been and a fantasy sprang immediately to mind that he'd chosen that particular chair deliberately, where he could see her.

She'd last felt that sense of excited anticipation in high school and the adrenalin rush sent happy shivers down her spine. So much for her resolve to keep things ordinary. One locked gaze with Nick Masters and she was putty in his hands. Sending a quick smile his way, she turned back to Philip on her left and her fantasies ground to a halt. Philip was not the sort to inspire fantasies. Philip was the sort of partner to make a girl think about a good, solid, respectable life of pre-dinner canapés and ladies who lunched for charity.

Was that the sort of dependable life she should be aiming for with the twins, a life where emotions were only ever on an even keel? Nothing spontaneous or unpredictable. Nothing exciting, or dangerous. And definitely nothing that encouraged images that drove every sane thought from her head.

She knew she should make the most sensible decision and turn the dance down. She should turn down anything Nick ever proposed. Although in one respect, it made no difference. She already knew she'd have fantasies aplenty to keep her tossing and turning tonight. And for some nights to come.

At the same moment the thought crossed her mind, a colleague of Philip's she knew reasonably well approached her and said with urgency, 'We need a doctor.'

Just what I was thinking, thought Rosie, but out loud she said, 'What is it?' And as she did, she knew instinctively she was waving goodbye to her plans for the rest of the evening.

CHAPTER FOUR

NICK watched as Rosie turned back to Philip. He didn't seem her type but, then, he didn't know her well. Besides, she'd ended things with him. He'd take that as proof he wasn't her type. It still begged the question as to why the guy would have let Rosie go without trying to juggle their lives somehow. Then again, what did it matter? Nick was the one Rosie had promised to dance with. Another man approached Rosie and bent down to talk to her. Nick bristled at the possibility that he'd been beaten to the first dance.

'Nick, mate.' Nick turned as a hand clasped his shoulder to find his friend Tim standing just behind his chair. 'We need a doctor.'

'What is it?' He listened as he glanced back at Rosie and found she was following the man who had spoken with her through the crowd. Same mission?

'The PM's Chief of Staff, Howard Hoffman, has collapsed, he's having trouble breathing,' Tim explained as he led the way across the room to a table where a rather overweight man, aged roughly in his fifties, sat slumped in a chair. Rosie was already there, loosening the man's tie. As Nick approached, he saw Howard's face was flushed and although at first glance he didn't look to be in any worse shape than most of the other ageing, overweight men in the room, he was audibly wheezing.

Nick said to Tim, his voice low, 'Has someone called an ambulance?'

'That was being done when I came to find you.'

'Check on it. We can always cancel it if we need to but it's better to be safe.'

'Will do.' Tim nodded and moved off to attend to it.

Nick joined Rosie and they acknowledged each other with a nod, a brief smile turning up the corners of Rosie's mouth for a moment. Then she said, 'Howard, Nick and I are doctors.' She gestured to Nick at her side and Howard glanced with glazed eyes at them both but gave no other sign of interest. 'Can you tell us if this has happened before?'

Rosie picked up the man's wrist, checking his pulse. As Howard nodded, Nick pushed Howard's other sleeve up, revealing a Medic Alert bracelet.

He read the inscription. 'Nut allergy.'

'Howard, do you have an epipen?' Rosie asked.

He nodded again.

'Where is it?'

'My wife,' Howard wheezed.

Nick and Rosie looked around at the same time but could see no one who looked like a concerned wife. Wouldn't she be coming forward?

'Where is she?' Nick asked.

'Bathroom,' Howard replied with difficulty. His lips had become more swollen, and soon he wouldn't be able to speak at all.

Rosie still had her fingers at the man's wrist. 'Pulse is more erratic,' she said to Nick. The redness on Howard's face was becoming worse, developing into hives now.

'Someone go and find her.' Nick spoke loudly, and the general noise around them quietened instantly. 'You.' He pinned his gaze on a woman hovering nearby. 'Check the ladies' bathrooms, we need that epipen.'

The woman didn't hesitate, clearly gathering from Nick's authoritative tone that time was of the essence. Thankfully Rosie was here, leaving him free for the time being to orchestrate events while Rosie attended to Howard.

Rosie was aware of Nick organising events, sending a woman to find the epipen, speaking to another man about an ambulance, leaving her free to concentrate on Howard. Getting a shot of epinephrine into him was really the only treatment but Rosie knew there were a couple of things she could do while they located Howard's wife. Calming Howard was one of them.

'We'll find your wife, Howard. Can you look at me and keep trying to breathe through your nose?' Rosie kept eye contact with Howard, keeping him focused on her. Keeping Howard's airway open was the priority for now as his breathing was becoming more laboured by the second.

'Does anyone have a Ventolin inhaler?'

Bronchodilators were normally not hard to find amongst a group of people of this size and one was quickly passed to Rosie.

'This will help you to breathe,' she said. 'Have you used one before?'

Howard nodded and Rosie held it for him, squeezing the cylinder four times, once for each of four inhalations. Nick was standing beside them, scanning the crowd.

'They've found her,' he said to Rosie.

'Howard? Howard!' Rosie could hear her now, coming closer.

'Make some space, let her through.' That was Nick.

A short, anxious-looking woman pushed through the crowd. She held the epipen in one hand, her handbag in the other. Rosie had no idea if Howard's wife planned to inject her husband but the woman's hands were shaking so badly Rosie wasn't going to let her try.

She took the epipen from the woman's fingers. 'I'm a doctor,

I can do it.' Howard's wife relinquished the pen and sank into the chair Nick pulled out for her.

'Thank you,' Rosie mouthed to Nick, who grinned at her, apparently confident she had the situation under control, although if she was the distractible type, his smile would have spelt the end of her efficiency. She popped the cap off the pen and held it against Howard's thigh. She depressed the button, plunging the adrenalin into his system while she counted to five.

'Do you find yourself in the middle of medical emergencies everywhere you go?' Nick had squatted down next to her, murmuring his words so only she could hear. 'First the accident at the beach, now this?'

'I was going to ask you the same thing.' She kept her eyes trained on Howard as they spoke. He was already responding positively to the drug, his breathing calming. 'The most dramatic thing I've come across off duty is some bad cases of sunburn. Perhaps it's our karma.'

'You don't have training in emergency medicine?'

'A GP with an interest in paediatrics?' She shook her head. 'Nothing so exciting there on a day-to-day basis.'

'Maybe—' Nick started to speak but was interrupted by someone in the crowd calling out that the ambulance was here.

Rosie saw people moving aside to let the paramedics through, and she and Nick stood up simultaneously. Whatever Nick had been going to say lost in the moment.

'Rosie?' Rosie jumped at the sound of Philip's voice behind her just as the paramedics arrived at Howard's side. She turned and motioned for him to wait while she filled the paramedics in on Howard.

That done, she left Nick with the paramedics and went to Philip.

'Well done with Howard. You averted some bad publicity there, thanks.'

Work was always Philip's first thought so she wasn't surprised his main concern was the negative coverage the event could have generated. 'There are some more people I want you to meet.'

Rosie considered her options. She'd promised to help Philip this evening. She could hardly refuse a direct request for help so she could dance with Nick instead. But she'd filled a fair quota of schmoozing with politicians and now she'd done some medical work on the side. Enough was enough...

'I might go home, Philip, I've had enough for one evening.'

'I understand.' Which he would. Philip was always courteous, to her, at least, even if he was unsure how to be so chivalrous to her niece and nephew. 'I'll get my driver to drop you.'

More chivalry. Nice, but not what she wanted. She wanted big and rugged, she wanted less polish and more manly command. She wanted Nick.

'I'll take a taxi.'

'If you're sure? I do appreciate your coming tonight; it wasn't the night I wanted to announce our separation.' He inclined his head slightly, a typical Philip gesture. 'This is nice, you and me still friends, still civil.'

Rosie laughed. 'It's one of the main things we have in common, Phil, civility at all costs. It's unlikely to desert us now.'

He bent to kiss her, aiming for her cheek this time. 'Let me know when you want to come down to Canberra to collect your things.'

'I will.' So it really was over. They'd both acknowledged it. Rosie waited for a pang of regret as Philip walked away but none came. Their relationship hadn't been right for her and becoming the twins' guardian had forced her to make the break that had already been a matter of when, not if. How different her life had become in a matter of weeks.

Politician's partner, Canberra, hobnobbing, black tie. Had

that been her? It felt a million miles away from where she was now. In just two months, the fit was no longer right.

Had it ever really been?

But the question hovering on her lips was, What was she going to be? Later on, when the dust had settled, where would she find herself?

Single female. Guardian aunt. Out-of-work doctor. Old Sydney girl come home for good. That was her, for now. And that was okay.

But later?

Sense of humour, attentive, intelligent, tall, gorgeous, safe-to-drown-in eyes, lover's hands…

She'd been looking for words to describe herself and a flood of words for Nick had come instead. She forced herself to stem the flow of descriptions. There was no room in her future for such an image. As if she held the same appeal for him as he did for her!

Then the image of tugging on his bow-tie until it tumbled loose about his neck swam back into mind and she let herself tumble with it, straight into a delectable daydream she really shouldn't be having in a public place.

The paramedics had left with Howard, and Nick had hung back until Philip had moved off, pleased when he saw Rosie scanning the crowd. He hoped she was looking for him, and as he stepped forward into her view, he knew from her smile his assumption had been correct.

'Well done with Howard.' He touched her on the arm and she moved ever so slightly closer to him, close enough for him to smell the light rose scent of her perfume, close enough to see she had exactly five golden freckles on the bridge of her nose. 'Does duty call or will we get our dance, more medical emergencies notwithstanding?'

'I think I have to go. Philip wanted me to meet more people

and I begged off on grounds of tiredness. And I should let Mum get home, she's babysitting.'

'All sound reasons but, even so, I'm disappointed.' She smiled at his teasing. 'I'll drive you home if you don't have a lift. My official duties as a token Kiwi are at an end.'

She hesitated then nodded and he did his best to look nonchalant and not as if his heart had been beating faster while he'd waited for her answer. She gave him her address but he knew it already. He knew they only lived a few streets apart, close to the hospital where he'd operate on Charlie. It was why he'd chosen that day for surgery, to make it easier for her.

'I'll say my goodbyes and meet you out the front, is that okay?'

'Sure,' she said, and they moved off in opposite directions.

Five minutes later he left the function room and scanned the foyer, his gut clenching when Rosie was at first nowhere to be seen. Then, through the doors, he caught a glimpse of yellow and saw she'd been waiting outside on the steps. The knots in his stomach relaxed.

They chatted easily on the walk to his car. Rosie's eyes widened as Nick slowed his steps when they approached an expensive-looking, sleek black car. She audibly swallowed a burst of laughter as Nick led her around the Mercedes Benz to his old heap obscured in the next parking bay. 'If I'd known I was driving you home, I'd have brought the Rolls.'

'I'm glad you didn't.' Rosie's green eyes danced with laughter. 'I've always had an aversion to Rolls-Royces.'

'Then you're going to love Molly,' he said patting the roof. 'She's about as far as something can be from a Rolls and still have an engine.' He opened the door for her, waiting for her to get settled before saying, 'Block your ears, this door needs quite a slam to get it shut.' She covered her ears with her hands, looking up at him with a big grin, and for a moment he simply stared at her, all golden and shining and beautiful and quite out of place in his car. Quite out of place in his world? After all, the movers and shakers they'd just spent the evening with were her world, not his.

Ten minutes later the conversation between them was still flowing naturally and he was still contemplating the question. And questioning why he cared. He was a single man with a single-minded focus on re-establishing himself. There were no plans for a relationship, even dating, in the next year or so. Yet as they chatted, bouncing off one another with their stories and laughter, he found himself returning again and again to the image of this gorgeous woman becoming a regular front-seat passenger in his car.

Impossible, but it made a pleasant change from thinking about work and debt all the time.

Curiosity got the better of him. 'How did you meet Philip?' His question was apropos of nothing but a quick glance her way suggested she wasn't taken aback so he went on, fishing, 'I wouldn't have thought a paediatrician would have much in common with a politician.'

'Some hospital function, a lifetime ago. He was the local Member of Parliament and an invited guest, I think.'

'You think?'

'I can't remember exactly. Is it important?'

'Sure it's important.'

'How?'

'Perhaps interesting is a better word than important. I love the idea of two people, when they're old and grey, being able to think back and remember the first moment they met. I think it's romantic.'

She considered that then nodded. 'I guess it is, but not for Philip and me, now that he's my ex-boyfriend.'

'Except you didn't know when you started going out with him that one day he'd be your ex.'

'Do you remember every ex-girlfriend and where you met?'

He laughed. 'Maybe there's one or two from years ago I'm

hazy about but, other than them, pretty much. I can even tell you when I first met you.' It wasn't something he'd meant to share, but he could hardly back away from the statement now. It was already out there. He'd just have to play down how well he recalled every detail about their first meeting.

She wasn't taking him seriously, anyway, and said laughingly, 'Not a real challenge, it was only a week ago and the circumstances were a little unusual.'

Despite his intentions to do the opposite, he rose to the challenge and raised the stakes. 'And I can tell you when I saw you for the second time.'

'A whole three days ago,' she teased, but he sensed now she was enjoying the exchange. Pleased she'd made an impression?

'Four days ago. And I remember what you were wearing.'

She nodded and gave a noncommittal 'Uh-huh.'

'A floaty top with some sort of pattern…' He paused as he negotiated a corner.

'So far so good.'

'In a green that matched your eyes.' He glanced over at her, pleased she was looking at him. It was hard to tell in the low light, but he was pretty sure a tinge of pink had crept up around her neck and her breathing was definitely shallower.

'Getting better.' She swallowed, and he had the feeling it was an effort for her to make her voice sound light, natural.

'And white pants with a stain on.' He visualised her that day. 'The left knee, where it looked like you'd spilled something.'

'I thought I'd got that stain out!'

'Not completely.'

'We'd had pancakes for breakfast and I spilt maple syrup. So either you've proved you've got a better memory for trivia than me, or you have a special interest in laundry.'

'Neither.' He let a moment of silence stretch between them. 'It proves I'm more interested in you than you were in Philip.' Man, there he went again. What was it about this woman that had him making such crazy admissions? He was straying so far from the script it was laughable.

'Oh.' The sound came out with a breath, making it sound husky. Desire hardened in his abdomen. Ah, that old chestnut. That was why he was acting so out of character. Desire he could cope with, he could stay in control of that. Only tonight he'd felt for the first time, like a physical sensation, that the noose around his neck had loosened. He was heading in the right direction. So he could loosen up, too, just a little, not a lot, right? Relax a little and spend some time with a woman who was attractive and interesting. He shut out the insistent voice that said it was more than that.

She was sitting still, staring at him. Wondering how to take what he'd just said? He looked back to the road, making a right turn into her street and slowing down to look at house numbers as he said, 'Which is perhaps not what you were expecting me to say but there it is. I'd like to spend some time with you. No pressure, no expectations.'

He pulled into her driveway, Rosie confirming with a gesture it was the right one. As he turned off the engine, she spoke.

'I'd really like that, Nick.' She hesitated and then went on, 'I'd really like to spend some time with you, too, as a friend, but my time's not my own at the moment. All my energy is going into the twins.'

Would she have said no if she wasn't responsible for the twins? Would she have interpreted the invitation as one of friendship if not for Lucy and Charlie? Yes, he'd already figured she wasn't the type for brief flirtations. Generally speaking, he didn't much go in for them either. But there were other ways to spend time together, ways that would work better for him, too, give him some company, some down time, without threatening his focus on work.

'I'm going to Campbell Parade for my regular Sunday

morning coffee around ten, probably followed with a stroll along the beach. Why don't you join me then, with the children? That way you don't need to choose between me or them and we're all happy.'

He could see her thinking this over, still wavering, still wary. 'Like I said, no pressure. We're both new here, it'd be nice to have some company.' Which was the truth, as far as it went. And given their claims to be looking for friendship, it was the most convenient truth.

'Nippers' training finishes at ten so, barring any other emergencies, we'll be getting our milkshakes from Marie just after.' She looked at him for confirmation.

'Excellent.' It was a tentative yes but he'd be happy with that. For now.

'So it's a date. Except it's not. A date.' She was stumbling a little with her words. 'Just friends, right?'

'Sure. Just friends.'

After that night, he would go over and over that moment. He remained adamant he'd meant every word of it when he'd spoken. Friends. But immediately afterwards he'd been hit with a sudden, almost overwhelming desire to unbuckle his seat belt and lean across to take her face between his palms and kiss her.

Soundly.

And nothing like 'just friends'.

But he'd said the words, 'Sure, just friends.' And he was a man who kept his word.

Besides, for every reason he wanted to kiss her there was another perfectly good reason why he shouldn't. Her mother was babysitting and probably waiting up, and he didn't want them to be caught on the front porch necking like a couple of teenagers. She was his patient's guardian and, not against the rules, but a little unorthodox. And he had no intention of getting seriously involved with any woman who might be a threat to his focus on rebuilding his career, a focus that was only just now paying off.

He followed his better judgment and got out of the car, walking around to Rosie's side and giving her his hand to help her out. Pulling her to her feet, there was a moment where they were standing very close, her hand still held in his, presenting a perfect opportunity to break his promise.

In the streetlight, he thought he detected a deeper blush on her cheeks. Her fingers were resting at her throat and he swore he could see the pulse point in her neck beating apace. No doubt about it, they were both aware of the chemistry between them. Maybe both regretting their claim of friendship moments before?

A car backfiring nearby broke the moment and Rosie looked down, opening her purse and taking out a key. 'Thanks for the lift. You don't need to walk me in, I'll be okay. See you tomorrow?'

He lifted a hand in farewell as Rosie stepped up to her front door, turning as she put her key in the lock and waved. Then she was gone.

Leaving him to contemplate whether they'd just missed an opportunity to experience something incredible or had had a lucky save.

Rosie closed the front door and leant back on it, giving herself a few moments to sort through her thoughts. She'd been so sure Nick had been about to kiss her that she'd almost closed her eyes in anticipation. Thank God she hadn't. She would have looked like a right twit.

Why had he waited?

Hadn't he wanted to kiss her as much as she'd wanted to be kissed? By him?

She should be glad he hadn't. Yet despite her claim that the twins were her priority, she wouldn't have protested if he'd taken her in his arms and kissed her.

But she should be grateful he hadn't. She had enough on her plate, a new relationship was not an option. Not that he'd been offering that. She was sure she'd read the subtext of his invitation correctly, sure she'd heard the fleeting suggestion of a fling. A vastly different proposition to a relationship. One she could manage? She thought of all the things she had to do, all the responsibilities mounting up daily.

If she didn't have the time or energy to get up to date with sorting bills, filing school notices and the laundry, she didn't have time for a fling.

But that wouldn't stop her imagination from filling in the blanks for her.

And for that, she thought as an image of Nick's lips at the exact moment she'd thought he was about to kiss her came into mind, she'd make time.

CHAPTER FIVE

NICK stretched his arms out wide before dropping them to his sides as he strode the last of the blocks before the beach, revelling in the freshness of the early morning, his favourite time of the day. A new day carried with it a feeling of promise, of possibility.

The sun was still low in the eastern sky, warming the pavement as he made his way to the coffee shop. The streets were relatively empty, although the crowds would soon start to appear for Sunday brunch. He'd checked on his hospital patients and now he could relax over coffee, something he always did after his swim, not before. He could always swim later, depending on what happened with Rosie and the twins. Missing one day didn't mean he was losing his focus. Even if today it wasn't his swim, or even his latte, he was looking forward to, as much as seeing Rosie.

Entering his regular coffee shop, which was, in fact, almost next to Marie's Milk Bar, he ordered before taking the Sunday paper to an outside table where Rosie would easily see him. From here, he had a good view of the beach. Nippers' training was coming to an end and the equipment was being packed away, so as the waitress delivered his coffee he took a guess and ordered a latte for Rosie before flicking through the paper.

The Sunday paper wasn't usually good for much except the

sport and television guide, but a story on page five caught his eye. He'd just finished reading it when he looked up to see Rosie and the children approaching. Pure. Fresh. Glowing. In fact, more relaxed than he'd seen her so far. Maybe the beach, barring medical emergencies, was where she felt happiest. A flicker of appreciation deep in his gut reflected his instant thought that she looked as good today as she had last night in that sun-yellow dress. That finely fitted, yellow dress that had figured prominently in his dreams last night. With her in it. Or out of it, depending on the stage of the dream.

He banished thoughts of his nocturnal preoccupations, and stood to greet them, saying hello to the children first. Lucy immediately stuck her hand out to shake his like they were old pals rather than having only met briefly once before. She was very unlike Charlie, in confidence at least. Meanwhile, Charlie stepped closer to Rosie but gave Nick a huge smile. Pleased with that, Nick winked at him but let him be.

He turned to Rosie, kissing her cheek, the softness of her skin beneath his lips taking him by surprise. She turned her face slightly as he kissed her other cheek, and her hair brushed lightly against his neck. His gut clenched as a half-remembered dream from only a few hours ago shimmered into focus. Rosie. Naked in his bed. Her hair loose over his chest as she lay across his body.

He closed his eyes briefly, shaking off the image that gave the lie to his claim of friendship only. This was Rosie, who had agreed only to spend some time with him. As friends. He wasn't sure she'd take too kindly to finding out she'd kept him tossing and turning, deliciously so, for the best part of last night.

'Morning, Nick.' She'd found her voice first. Luckily, the twins were preoccupied with the cartoon section of the paper he'd left on the table and hadn't noticed the taut silence between the grown-ups.

It was then he noticed her footwear and laughed out loud,

restoring the ease that had been between them before he'd steered them off course last night with his thinly veiled proposal. She was smiling as she followed his gaze down to her feet. 'I see you're impressed with Lucy's choice of shoes for me.' At the mention of her name, Lucy looked up from the comic strips.

'Very becoming.' He nodded, keeping a straight face for Lucy's sake. The bright green flip-flops were each resplendent with an enormous plastic yellow flower attached to the rubber strap between Rosie's toes. 'Fascinating choice, Lucy.' The little girl beamed at the praise and took a step closer to their new friend. Nick gestured at the chairs around his table. 'Would you like to join me?'

'It'll be the end to your peaceful morning,' said Rosie, but she wasn't making any effort at a real protest.

'Peace and quiet I can get any time but the company of three such wonderful people is hard to come by. Besides, I've ordered you a coffee.'

'What sort did you order?' Lucy piped up. 'Rosie is very fussy about her coffee.'

'Is she now?' Nick pretended to consider Lucy's concern seriously. 'I ordered a latte. How did I do?'

'You got it right,' said Lucy.

Rosie added, 'She's right, I am fussy about coffee but after such a late night and an early start today, I think I'd eat the coffee straight from the tin.' Rosie smiled and the Bondi sun paled by comparison.

'Why don't you two go and get your milkshakes from Marie next door and bring them back here?' Rosie said as she handed Lucy some money. The twins ran off, happy with the responsibility, and Rosie settled in the chair he had pulled out for her.

'Have you seen the paper?' he asked as he sat down again.

'Not for the past two months!' She laughed. 'It gets delivered and week after week goes in the recycling before I get to it. Why?'

'You're in it.'

'What?'

Nick opened the paper up to page five, folding the pages back on themselves so it didn't take over the table, and passed it to Rosie, tapping the article. 'There.'

He waited while Rosie read the short article, watching as her lips moved silently as she perused the paper. He was interested to hear her comments on one remark in particular.

She read a sentence out loud. 'Mr Philip Garrett said, "It was lucky for the PM's Chief of Staff that my partner was here. Dr Jefferson saved his life, her quick actions..." Not just lucky for Howard, lucky for Philip, too,' she commented drily.

'What do you mean?'

'That's one way to get his name in the paper.'

'You don't mind that he used your goodwill for self-promotion?' Nick asked curiously.

She shook her head, seemingly unperturbed, which surprised him. He'd really expected her to be offended, to feel she'd been used. Did she think using other people to make opportunities for oneself was acceptable? If so, even this friendship caper wasn't going to work out. He waited for her to explain more.

'It goes with the job. He even thanked me last night for averting bad publicity. Although in Phil's opinion, there's no such thing as bad press. It's better to have his name in the paper for any reason than to be forgotten about.' She stopped suddenly and added, 'That sounds uncharitable, but it's not meant to be. It's not just Philip who is like that. It's the nature of politics, I think.'

If she wasn't going to comment on the part that was bothering him, he'd just have to come straight out and ask.

'What about him claiming to be your partner?'

She shrugged. 'He would have done that to give more weight to his comments. Why would the journalist bother to interview him otherwise? They could have interviewed any number of people but I guess, as my date, he would seem like a more desirable witness, thereby getting his name in the paper for an event that he wasn't involved in. Clever, really.'

'Clever?' Nick's hopes even for a friendship were being tested.

'Sure, if you need publicity like you need air, you either hope you have a knack for generating it or you have to learn to take your opportunities. Philip has a knack, he's good at it.' Nick's heart had sunk about as low as his first cup of coffee. 'Personally, I can't think of a worse way to have to live my life and I realised that anew last night.'

'In what way?' His heart was tentatively creeping back up into his chest.

'When I was with Philip I was happy to support him but it's not my thing, I don't enjoy the networking. But it was important to him, and I understood why.'

'Which is why you helped him out by going last night?'

She nodded. 'And why I'm now thrilled I've done my duty and I don't have to be part of that world any more.' She was flicking through the paper as she spoke, apparently unfazed by the idea of Philip moving on. At this sequence of announcements, Nick's heart lodged firmly back where it should be.

The twins returned, slurping noisily on their straws, concentrating on their treat. Rosie was now pulling the paper apart. 'Do you mind if I take this bit out?' She pulled out the sports section and held it up to him.

'No, go for it.'

She folded up the remainder of the paper and put it to one side, passing the sports pages to Charlie, who immediately turned to the cricket section.

'Do you like cricket, Charlie?'

He looked at Nick and nodded and Nick was pleased to see that Charlie kept eye contact. He'd spent a bit of time over the past couple of days refreshing his knowledge of selective mutism, checking up new advances and any new theories. Charlie didn't show signs of withdrawing completely and Nick was determined to work on gaining his young patient's trust.

'The Tri-Nations One Day Series is about to start. I'm from New Zealand originally. Do you think we can beat the Aussies this year?'

Charlie shook his head vigorously and Nick grinned. 'You're probably right, but we'll have a good go.'

'Hey, you live here now, shouldn't you be barracking for Australia?' Rosie teased.

'I'm not an Australian citizen yet. I'll support the Aussies when they play against anyone else, but not against the Kiwis. My family would disown me.'

'Do you go to the cricket?'

'I always plan to, but I never quite seem to make it.'

A loud slurping sound interrupted their conversation. 'Lucy!' Rosie remonstrated.

'Sorry,' Lucy replied, looking anything but. 'That was the best milkshake.' She leant across the table, peering into Rosie's glass. 'Have you finished your coffee yet? Remember you said we could go to the Smiggle shop to get a present for Emma.'

'Who or what is a Smiggle?' Nick asked, imagining a new type of furry toy.

'It's a stationery shop.'

'Yeah, they have really cool stuff,' Lucy added.

Rosie saw Charlie roll his eyes. 'It's okay, Charlie, we'll be quick.'

'Where is this shop?' Nick asked.

Rosie pointed north. 'Up that way.'

'That's my direction.' It wasn't, but it could just as easily be. His swim fell further off his list of activities for the day and he found he didn't care if it meant more time with Rosie. 'I'll walk with you.'

She hesitated, meeting his gaze and holding it for a moment.

He couldn't read the look in her eyes but she seemed to be mulling the offer over. Was she doubting his claim of friendship? She nodded and he grinned, reaching across the table to gather the rest of the paper.

She was hesitating and she didn't know why. Since she didn't have an answer, she nodded. It was what she wanted, after all. More time with Nick, and he looked genuinely happy with her decision, a thought that made her feel good. She reached across the table to gather the scattered sports pages and Nick must have had the same thought as his hand came down on top of hers and she froze as her heart skipped a beat. She forgot what she'd been doing, totally absorbed by the touch of his hand. Looking up at him, she was afraid her desire would be written all over her face, but there was small chance she could change that.

Nick ran his thumb over the back of her hand before he moved away, leaving a trail of heat across her skin. It had all happened so quickly she could have imagined it, just like the moment last night when she'd thought he'd been about to kiss her. Glancing at the twins confirmed they'd noticed nothing unusual, even Charlie, who was highly observant, largely thanks to his mostly silent existence. Rosie snatched her hand off the table, holding it in her lap, breathing rapidly, leaving Nick to fold the papers.

She pushed her chair back and stood up, needing to move. 'Let's walk along the esplanade.' Her speech was flustered.

Seemingly unfazed, Nick fell into step beside her as the children raced each other along the esplanade, leaving the two of them in their wake. She took a deep breath, willing herself to be as together as he was. Easy, she told herself, all I need to do is control my hormones and stop having imaginary meaningful moments with my nephew's specialist.

'The three of you seem to be doing well.' He'd stuck his hands in his pockets, a picture of nonchalance. 'They're lovely children.'

'We have our moments, although I seem to be having more of those than the children. Being a full-time carer is very different from having them for a few hours. I feel I'm being split in half a lot of the time. Other than Nippers, they don't do the same things. They have different interests and I can't please them both at the same time.'

'Is it even possible?'

She shrugged. 'I don't know. None of my friends have children, they're all busy with their careers, so I'm flying blind a lot of the time.'

'I've got twelve nieces and nephews. I'm sure between them they've created every scenario known to man, so if you need any information, just ask.'

'I think our situation is a little out of the ordinary. The kids have to deal with losing both their parents and with Charlie's mutism on top of that.'

'It's a big load, there's no argument, but don't forget I'm your new Sydney buddy and if I can help, I'm happy to. And speaking as Charlie's specialist for a moment, I've got hold of the expert on selective mutism in the States since Charlie's last consult. She's reassured me that the fact Charlie talks to you, while it puts more of a burden on you, is a highly protective factor. As long as he's got someone to talk to and, don't forget, he also talks to Lucy and your parents, he has a way of expressing his feelings. He's not bottling things up because of his mutism so don't attribute problems to him any more than you would to Lucy.'

He took her hand in his and gave it a light squeeze as if it was the most natural of gestures between friends, before letting it go again as if it was just that, a gesture of comfort between friends. He wasn't to know his touch gave her palpitations and had her thinking thoughts not fit for the responsible guardian of two young children.

'Besides, I think we had a mini-moment of progress at the

last appointment.' He filled her in on Charlie's note and boiled-lolly present.

'Really?' She'd been thrilled at the coffee shop to see Charlie interacting happily with Nick. Now, even though it was a long shot, part of her hoped that perhaps Charlie was nearer a breakthrough than even his psychologist thought. Just how integral would Nick be to a breakthrough?

'All up, it looks to me you're doing pretty well. You know Charlie can speak, he just mostly chooses not to. It will come with time. Just make sure you don't give him excuses or reasons not to talk. Don't let the accident with his parents become an excuse for his mutism. Treat him the same way you treat Lucy.'

'Thank you, I'll try to do that.' They walked in silence for a moment or two, Rosie trying not to read anything into the fact that their strides were perfectly matched—length, speed, they were all in place. 'Does that count as a scheduled consult?'

He laughed. 'Consider it a gift between friends.'

They caught up to the children then. Lucy was on the swing in the playground and Charlie was perched on the sea wall, watching a game of beach cricket.

'The shop's just there,' said Rosie, gesturing to the stationery shop right across the road.

'Charlie, what say you and I see if they need a few more beach cricketers? Sounds better than shopping, right?'

Charlie didn't hesitate, nodding vigorously and looking to Rosie for permission.

Nick seemed to have the magic touch as far as Charlie was concerned.

And as for her? She knew the answer, not that it made a jot of difference to anything she'd do.

She stood watching the man and boy head down to the sand. Nick looked back over his shoulder. He called back to her, shaking his head at her, laughter in his eyes, 'Charlie and I'll be fine doing some bloke stuff. Just meet us on the beach when you're done. No hurry.'

And that was it. Off they went, Charlie trotting beside Nick as if they did this every Sunday. Not even a backward glance.

Just how magic was this man, to have worked such a miracle of trust in Charlie in such a short space of time?

Rosie expected that by the time Lucy had made her decisions in the stationery shop the boys would be ready to call it quits but the game was still in full swing and Charlie was in the thick of it. Silent, but participating. Lucy sat in the sand admiring her purchases and writing in Emma's birthday card, leaving Rosie free to sit in the sun and watch the game. She told herself she wasn't joining in because she didn't want to intrude on Charlie's male bonding time but she knew it was really because, sitting here hidden behind her sunglasses, she was free to look where she liked.

And she liked to look at Nick.

It was Charlie's turn to bowl and Nick was giving him some tips, bending down beside Charlie, his knees slightly bent with his hands resting on his thighs. His boardshorts were pulling taut across his hips and Rosie admired the view she had from behind. The fabric of his T-shirt was stretched across his back and she could imagine the ripple of muscles running from his shoulder blades to his hips. He stood up, returning to his position as Charlie ran in to bowl.

To say Charlie's first ball was a little wide would be too kind but Nick praised his effort and then directed him to bowl from the other side of the wickets.

The next ball was much better and the batter connected, hitting it right in the middle of his bat, sending it hurtling through the air. Nick took off, his muscled calves pumping as he ran through the soft sand towards the ball. He dived to his right and caught the ball mere inches above the ground.

He leapt to his feet, one hand held above his head in cele-bration, before he ran to Charlie, giving him a big high five. Charlie slapped his palm against Nick's, not at all self-con-scious about the attention. In fact, he was smiling more widely than Rosie had seen him do for a long while.

Rosie joined in the cheers and Charlie turned his smile on her, as carefree as any ordinary eight-year-old. Nick turned, fol-lowing Charlie's gaze, made their excuses to the beach team and headed over to her, Charlie padding by his side.

'You were great, Charlie. Terrific bowling.'

'What about my catch?' Nick asked, dusting sand from the front of his shorts.

Rosie struggled to keep her focus on his face and away from his hands. She stood up, bringing herself to a higher, less vulnerable position. 'Not bad.' Pretty darned good, actually, but she wasn't brave enough to say that.

'Charlie and I make a pretty good team.'

Charlie nodded his agreement.

'You do, but I'm afraid that's it for today, Charlie. We've got to get Lucy to Emma's party.'

'I had a great time, thanks, Charlie. We'll do it again another day.'

Nick shook Charlie's hand and, again, Charlie made eye contact with Nick. The nephew appeared as smitten by Nick's charm as the aunt. Rosie waved Lucy over and they retraced their steps along the esplanade, the twins racing ahead once again.

'Slow down, you two, you'll trip if you're not careful,' Rosie called after them, but the children sprinted off as if they hadn't heard her.

'Would you like to catch up during the week, just the two of us, maybe see a movie, have a bite to eat? You know.' His grin was electric and full of cheek. 'Two friends hanging out?'

Rosie's heart did a slow somersault in her chest, feeling like it collided with every other organ on its rotation. This time she didn't doubt her instincts. He'd tagged the 'friends' comment on again but the look in his eyes gave his words deeper meaning. This time she was prepared to bet he was as attracted to her as she was to him. The 'friends' tag was a cover for both of them, giving them a way to get to know each other with no expectations, or because he had no intention of a real involvement. But did that matter? He wanted to spend time with her. She had a friend. And for the first time since she'd moved to Sydney, maybe even for quite a while before that, she felt like she was coming to life again, as if Nick was pouring precious water on the lonely, parched earth her life had become.

But it was precious water she'd have to forgo this time.

'I'd love to but I'm already going out on Tuesday night. I'm meeting my girlfriend. I don't want to ask Mum to help out more than once a week.' This was the first time she'd actually seen her friend Alison for anything other than a quick coffee since she'd got to Sydney. The first time she'd been out properly, in fact, other than the dinner last night. Just her luck! She wouldn't be going at all if it wasn't for the fact Ally had begged for her support. Why did doing the right thing by others always seem to equate to her missing out? Maybe this time it didn't have to? 'Can I take a rain check?'

'No problem. Just let me know the next time you have a free night.'

'I—' Rosie's reply came to an abrupt halt as she saw Charlie go sprawling across the footpath up ahead. 'Charlie!' She ran towards him as fast as her inappropriate footwear would let her. Flip-flops were not made for running.

Nick overtook her and by the time she reached the children Charlie was sitting up, looking at the blood gushing from his skinned knees and palms. Tears were welling in his eyes but she could see he was trying to be brave. Lucy was crouched beside him.

Rosie knelt down and scooped Charlie onto her lap, wrapping him in her arms. 'You'll be okay, Charlie. I know it hurts.'

Charlie's shoulders were shaking with silent sobs as tears ran down his cheeks. Even his crying was done in silence when he was in public.

Rosie's first instinct was to get him home so she could clean his grazes but Lucy had other ideas.

'You need to sing to him. Sing him the song Mum always sings when we get hurt.'

Lucy was talking about her mum in the present tense. Rosie had no clue about the song. Her confusion must have been written on her face.

'You know, the one about the mockingbird.'

She knew it, and she started to sing, conscious of Nick standing beside her family as they knelt on the footpath. When she paused, searching for the half-remembered words.

Lucy prompted her, joining in with her little-girl lilt.

As they sang in unison Charlie's sobs finally subsided as he wiped his eyes. Rosie held him close, nestling her face into the warm curve of his neck, before helping him to his feet.

'It'll be okay,' she said to both the children, hoping she would be proved right. She was talking more about their lives in general than about Charlie's grazed knees. 'Do you think you can walk? We'd better get you home and patched up.'

Charlie nodded. His grazes would be painful but they weren't deep. If she could distract him, he wouldn't have any trouble getting home.

'Will you be okay with them both?' Nick asked.

'Sure.' Knowing he was about to leave them, she wished she could ask for his help, just to extend the morning, but she didn't really need his assistance. And she probably wouldn't have asked even if she had needed it.

He laid his hand on her upper arm, his touch on her bare skin delicious. 'Sure?' He smiled, his eyes crinkling at the corners in the way she already loved.

She nodded, the touch of his hand rendering her speechless. For one delicious moment she thought he was going to lean in and kiss her goodbye. But the moment passed and suddenly he was saying a hearty farewell to the twins. As he turned to go, he tipped an imaginary hat to Rosie and said quietly, his voice deep and rich and satisfying to her ears, 'I think I should warn you, I have a thing for girls who can sing.'

And then he gave her a wink that left her unsure if he'd been teasing or flirting, but either way it made her whole body tingle and the feeling stayed with her for the rest of the day.

CHAPTER SIX

ROSIE took a deep breath and pushed open the gallery doors. Going to events on her own was not her forte, especially when she'd been out of circulation for so long. It was silly but it would be easier to turn around and head for home.

Her apprehension settled when she found Alison, as small and dark as Rosie was tall and fair, standing just inside the main gallery, greeting guests.

'Hi,' she said, stretching up to kiss Rosie on both cheeks. 'Thanks for coming. The other girls aren't here yet. Grab a glass of bubbly and stay with me for a bit while I say hello to a few people.'

A waitress handed Rosie a drink and she picked up a catalogue and flicked through it while Alison switched back and forth between chatting to her and greeting guests.

'The exhibition is a collaboration between emerging indigenous artists from Australia and New Zealand. There are some incredible works. If you're smart, you could pick up a few great investments.'

'Who would you recommend?' Not that she would be purchasing anything. Taking leave without pay from work didn't fit with splashing out on art, no matter how great it was.

'There's a young Aboriginal artist whose paintings are on the end of this wall.' Alison waved her hand down the room.

'He's worth a look,' she said as she handed a catalogue to another couple as they walked past. 'And there are some stunning woodcarvings by a New Zealand artist just next to that. Her bio is on page fifteen.'

Rosie glanced down, flicking through the pages. She hadn't yet found the page when Alison nudged her in the ribs and spoke in a smoky murmur that alerted Rosie that her friend had spotted some talent. 'Have a look at what just walked in. Remember, if he's straight, I saw him first.'

Rosie looked up and had no trouble spotting which good-looking guy her friend was talking about. 'Get in line, Ally, I'll introduce you.'

'You know him?' Ally gave her a sideways glance. 'You're a dark horse. Have you been refusing my invites because you've been secretly canoodling with that lovely gentleman?'

'Yes, I know him, but there's been no canoodling.'

'But you want to, right? And if you don't, can I go to the front of the line?' Alison was practically hanging off Rosie's arm, imploring her friend to play nice.

'Shh,' muttered Rosie just as Nick caught sight of her past the few people standing between them.

'Rosie!' Nick walked towards her, breaking into a huge grin. As usual, his smile went straight to the core of her, igniting her senses and all but melting her insides. 'So this is your mysterious Tuesday night function.' He laid a hand on her arm and kissed her on the cheek, just as she'd imagined he was going to do at the beach. He did it so easily, so naturally, as if he'd done the same thing a hundred times, no big deal, whereas she'd been imagining the moment over and over since Sunday.

It was only the softest brush of his lips but she knew how right she'd been to anticipate it and she savoured the touch of his mouth, a flare of heat flashing over her skin. If this was a chaste kiss on the cheek, what magic would his mouth work on her lips?

She wanted to know.

Soon.

Alison cleared her throat, bringing Rosie back to reality.

Rosie resisted the urge to shake her head to clear her mind, surprised to find her hand was on Nick's arm. She must have reached out automatically as he'd kissed her. She covered her surprise by giving him a little tap as if that was why she'd touched him in the first place, before removing her hand to gesture to Ally. 'Nick, this is my friend Alison. She manages the gallery.'

'Alison, it's a great set-up you've got here.' Nick shook her hand. Cool, calm, collected. How much she wanted to affect him as he did her. She knew she couldn't get involved, her focus had to be on the twins, not on her own desires, but how wonderful it would feel to know she had the option.

She watched as Ally looked Nick up and down and felt a tweak of satisfaction when she saw the look of appreciation in her friend's eyes. She knew Ally was taking in every detail of Nick's appearance and, if asked afterwards, her artist's eye would recall everything.

It was worth recalling.

His outfit, black jeans and shirt, wasn't dissimilar to what a dozen other men in the room were wearing. But none wore their clothes as well as Nick. His jeans, slightly faded, hugged his hips and his shirt fitted him so well it looked as though it had been handmade for him. His shirt was untucked and his hair was a little unruly. He looked perfectly at home, more like one of the artists than one of the invited corporate suits that he must be. She, on the other hand, despite being a veteran of opening nights thanks to her years with Philip, was never quite sure she'd chosen the right outfit. The only thing that saved her was her slim build and height, which meant clothes tended to hang well on her.

'Nice meeting you, Nick. If you'll excuse me, there are a

few people I need to schmooze with. Will you look after Rosie while I do the rounds?' Ally had finished giving Nick the once-over and clearly felt he was worth Rosie's spending time with.

'It would be my pleasure.'

Ally left with good grace, though not before she'd managed to mouth to Rosie behind Nick's back, 'He's a keeper,' and given her a thumbs-up.

Rosie pretended she'd seen nothing as she asked Nick, 'What are you doing here?'

'I take it it's not where you'd expect to find me.'

'I guess not. I wouldn't have picked you as an art lover. I can see you at the beach, the cricket, saving lives. But art exhibitions?' She rocked her hand in the air to indicate her ambivalence. 'Not so much.'

'I know how to appreciate beautiful things...' He paused as his eyes scanned her face. 'As well as the next cultural aficionado.' His tone was enough to make her face warm even if the heat of his glance hadn't made his meaning clear.

She stuck with the literal interpretation of his comment. She had no idea how to respond to the other, more personal message. 'So you go to a lot of art shows?'

He laughed. 'No, you're right, it's not really my thing. An old friend from New Zealand is in town for work, this is his only free evening and he wanted to come here, so this is where we're catching up. James works in Perth now, we don't see each other often.'

'Was there something special he wanted to see here tonight?'

Nick cleared his throat, looking a little uncomfortable. 'Someone we know has some work exhibited. James was keen to come and since his time is tight, we thought we'd start here.' He glanced around the room. 'He should be along any minute.'

Rosie was sure he'd just changed the subject but not at all sure why he would need to.

'Shall we take a stroll and have a look?' Nick took her hand in his and again, as he touched her, her sense of touch went into overdrive and she lost the power of speech. She nodded and he led her through the gallery.

They wandered past the artworks, stopping in front of the Aboriginal artist's paintings Alison had mentioned, but it was the wooden carvings beside these that caught her eye, a pair of mermaids, each about a foot long, carved out of shiny, dark brown wood. Their tails were inlaid with mother-of-pearl shell that caught the light, glistening as the mermaids reclined on the display stand.

Nick was still focusing intently on the paintings. Too intently, Rosie got the feeling. Again, she couldn't quite figure out why. She let go of his hand and moved on just a metre to admire the mermaids but a life-size carving of a nude male then caught her attention.

The figure was carved from a lighter wood, giving it a realistic shine. It was so warm and lifelike she reached out, intending to run her hands over it, stopping when she realised what she was about to do and stealing a guilty glance about her. She wasn't sure of the etiquette but didn't imagine it was the done thing to touch artworks, especially when the subject was naked.

When her gaze settled on Nick, she found he'd emerged from his reverie in front of the painting and was looking in her direction. Had he seen her about to touch the figure?

Then she realised he was hardly aware of her and was looking at the carving, seeming somewhat bewildered. Was he doubting her artistic taste, admiring a naked man?

He gave her a brief nod, in an absent-minded fashion, before turning back to the painting. She would have gone back to his side but she was mesmerised by the carving. She checked the artist's name and flicked through the catalogue, compelled to find out more. She wasn't surprised to find the information on page fifteen. The artist was one of the two Alison had recommended. She was reading the biography next to a picture of the artist, a stunning dark-haired woman who looked mighty happy with herself, when a voice made her look up.

'Nikolai!'

Nikolai? The slight pained expression that crossed Nick's features told her that wasn't his full name but an affectation on the stranger's part. Rosie didn't recognise the slim, blond man walking towards them but Nick clearly did. Rosie wasn't at all sure Nick was happy to see him. The undercurrents she'd sensed with Nick over the last minutes deepened.

The man was by Nick's side, draping a hand over Nick's shoulder, leaning in to kiss him on both cheeks.

Nick seemed to be standing rigid and he simply stated, 'Paulo,' by way of greeting. The feeling of tension wasn't dissipating.

'What a surprise to see you.' Paulo stressed the 'you'. He waved a hand to indicate the carvings. 'Blast from the past, yes? Miriam will be titillated to hear you were here.'

Rosie looked back at the catalogue in her hand, recalling the name. Miriam Te Rito, the artist. There was a photo, showing a tall, striking woman, her Maori lineage evident in the gorgeous creamy, caramel colour of her skin and the black hair falling past her shoulders in a shiny swathe. Was it just her imagination or was the woman exuding sexual energy even from the photo? Or was Rosie just picking up on the tensions simmering in Nick?

Pretty clearly, Miriam Te Rito was the artist Nick and his friend knew. The way he'd mentioned her, though, hadn't implied there was anything out of the ordinary. The way he'd been acting since he'd seen the carvings and now since Paulo had arrived suggested something more.

With Paulo draped over him, Nick remained as stiff as a board while Paulo chirped a series of inanities that required no real answer from the man he was persistently calling Nikolai.

There were serious undertones going on here and she had no idea what they meant, except that Nick clearly wasn't comfortable. Now Paulo seemed to notice Rosie for the first time. And, more importantly, that Rosie was standing with the catalogue opened to the page with Miriam. He disentwined himself from Nick and stepped over to her.

'You like Miriam's work?' His tone was confident, seemingly friendly, but again Rosie was sure there was a calculated desire to cause trouble behind the friendly façade.

'She's very talented. This one in particular is fabulous.' She turned her attention back to the figure of the naked male, keen to disengage from Paulo.

The sculpted figure was lying on his side, facing the wall, one arm under his head, the other thrown across his face as if shielding it from the sun. The wood had a rosy glow and the sculpture gleamed in the light. The broad shoulders tapered into a narrow waist, continuing down into perfectly shaped, tight buttocks before the sculpture ended mid-thigh.

'This is one of her best pieces.' His tone was self-satisfied and Rosie waited for something more from him, some sort of dig at her, but he turned his back on her. Maybe he'd got what he wanted from their brief exchange? He turned back to Nick, effectively excluding Rosie and chatting just to Nick so Rosie couldn't hear.

With Paulo's eyes off her, Rosie gave in to temptation. Unable to resist any longer, despite knowing she would be betraying just how much she liked the piece, she reached out and ran a hand along the smooth curve of the man's hip. Running her fingers up to the waist, she lingered, feeling the satin of the smooth wood under her fingers. The wood was warm to touch, adding to the lifelike appearance.

'You can see she had—' Paulo had once again swivelled to face Rosie, including her again, and a flicker of a smile appeared when he saw Rosie touching the piece of art. 'You can see she had an ideal model.' Paulo paused a moment, and

Rosie instinctively knew it was for effect. He wanted Rosie's full attention before he spoke again. 'Nikolai, be a darling and turn around, see if Rosie can see the resemblance.'

Rosie snatched her hand away from the sculpture as though it had self-combusted. She stared at Nick. 'This is *you*?'

He nodded, looking increasingly uncomfortable at the way things were going. Paulo's gaze darted back and forth from Rosie to Nick, his smirk making it clear he was enjoying the impact he was making.

'It's good, isn't it? It's taken me a long time to convince her to be able to part with it.' He touched Nick on the arm. 'That would come as no surprise to you, Nikolai, given what you love-birds shared, but Miriam could no longer resist the sort of money this will fetch in Sydney.'

A thousand questions sprang to Rosie's mind. Before she could ask any of them a short, very effeminate man bustled up to them and interrupted. 'Paulo darling, come, there's someone you need to meet.'

Paulo was whisked away, winking at Rosie as he left, leaving the two of them standing in silence.

For a good sixty seconds neither of them spoke, then Nick let out a soft whistle.

'I'd have to say,' he said, his tone dry, 'that was one of the more awkward moments of my life.'

He'd managed to lighten the moment, enough for Rosie to try out her voice despite knowing her cheeks were still burning.

'You're embarrassed?' She forced herself to look at Nick as if she wasn't ready to crawl under the nearest installation and spend the rest of the evening hidden. 'At least you knew it was you and didn't stand here like a twit admiring it.' She bit her lip. 'Should I apologise for touching it?'

'Touching?' The grin he sent was lopsided, teasing and much too appealing. He'd recovered his equilibrium a lot quicker than she had. 'I think caressing longingly would be a more accurate description.

'Tell you what,' he went on, when she found herself speechless with embarrassment, 'this is not the most relaxing situation for either of us. Let's go for a walk. I'll give James a call and meet him in an hour or so. In the meantime, I think I've got some explaining to do. Besides,' he added, his cheeky grin widening, 'I need to get out of here, I'm not used to having my naked butt on full public display.'

She laughed at that, starting to relax at the mere prospect of getting out of there, away from Paulo and away from Nick's perfect rear, or at least another woman's representation of that part of his anatomy.

Rosie made her excuses to Ally, who squealed at the thought Rosie was leaving early with her hot man. At the front door she found Nick waiting for her, two glasses of champagne in his hand.

He handed one to Rosie as they left the gallery, saying, 'Tonight, we've suffered for the sake of art. Consider this our compensation.'

Just outside, away from the din, Nick rang James, and Rosie stood pondering what tonight really meant. Especially the neon-bright question: when had Nick posed for Miriam? And why?

'James is fine with that.' Nick came to her side and slung his arm around her for a moment, leading her away from the gallery. The sun had set but the night was still warm and the scent of frangipani was heavy in the air.

Together they walked where Nick led, crossing the road, heading towards the cliffs on the eastern side of Sydney's South Head.

'Where are we going?'

'Macquarie's Lighthouse. I guarantee there will be neither ex-partners, mine at least, nor naked sculptures there.'

The whitewashed lighthouse buildings were silhouetted

against the darkness of the night and a curtain of stars draped across the sky as a background. A wooden bench sat just inside the cliff-top fence and Rosie perched on the backrest, her feet on the seat, Nick dropping onto the seat by her side. The smell of the sea drifted up from far below the cliffs and as she took a sip of her drink, the yeasty aroma of champagne filled her senses, replacing the salty tang of the sea.

'For the record, I had no idea Paulo was going to be there tonight. James told me Miriam wouldn't be there but I didn't think about Paulo. He's been Miriam's agent for years but it didn't occur to me he'd come across from New Zealand for the opening. Even if I'd known, I wouldn't have thought much of it but it seems he was in the mood for trouble tonight. I also had no idea she still had the...' Words seemed to escape him for the first time. 'Still had the...'

'Carving.'

'That's the one.'

'Yes. The One.' In her mind, she capitalised the piece of art that seemed now to stand as a barrier between them. 'When did you sit for her?'

'Years ago, before we were married.'

She'd just taken a sip of champagne and she choked on the bubbles, her throat stinging as she swallowed the mouthful too sharply. 'You're *married*?' This was going from bad to worse. She was filled with a sensation which she suspected was jealousy and the champagne bubbles stung her nose.

'Not now, we're divorced.'

He seemed unflustered, her discomfort emphasising his calmness.

She scrutinised him through narrowed eyes. He didn't look like the sort of man to be with the sort of woman she was sure Miriam was. For one thing, Miriam looked older than Nick. By quite a lot. And she looked hard. Self-interested, too. All that from a photo? Rosie quizzed herself. She conjured up the image in the photo again. Yes. She was sure of it. What would have brought them together?

She summarised those thoughts with a simple statement: 'You don't look divorced.'

'Tell me.' Nick was smiling up at her, the tension evident in him earlier seeming to have disappeared the moment Paulo had. 'How does a divorcé look?'

At that, Rosie turned her hands palms up. She didn't have the first idea what she meant by that. What she really meant was he didn't look like he'd have married a woman like Miriam in the first place, but she could hardly say that. Could she?

He went on when she drew a blank. 'I promise I'm divorced. I have been for two years.'

'But she still has the carving?' Somehow the carving was at the nexus of what was bothering her.

'It looks that way. But what you're really asking,' he continued, precisely reading her unasked question, 'is why.' She nodded and he said, 'You like it.' He grinned at his thinly veiled reference to her clear appreciation of the piece. 'Maybe she does too.'

Rosie resisted the urge to kick him for his light-hearted answer but couldn't suppress a smile. There was a funny side to the chain of events of tonight, even if she wasn't quite seeing the humour in it yet as much as he was.

'Listen,' he said as he raised himself up until he, too, was sitting on the back of the wooden bench. 'I shouldn't tease. I'm just trying to make the best of it.'

Rosie shook her hair back from her face, feigning a nonchalance she didn't feel. 'It's fine. I'm j-just a little embarrassed that I—I was running my fingers over you,' she stuttered, and corrected herself, 'it, in front of you, not knowing.'

'Don't be, I'm flattered. It's not every day I get to watch a beautiful woman stroke my—'

Rosie held up a hand, cutting him off, before hiding her face behind her hands as she spoke. 'Don't say it, don't, I'm only just coping now.' Which was true, but embarrassment was only part of what was eating at her.

None of this was a big deal. It didn't matter he was divorced. It shouldn't matter she'd just been stroking a life-size, naked representation of him right in front of him.

True, that was embarrassing. Cringe-worthy, in fact, but nothing she couldn't cope with.

It also shouldn't matter that the carving had been created when he and Miriam had been involved.

But there she came unstuck because it did matter. A lot.

Why? It was proof positive Miriam had affected him in a way Rosie had been daydreaming of doing. She didn't think for a moment that Nick was harbouring regrets and wishes of reunions with his ex. She didn't know how she knew that— body language, woman's intuition—but she knew it just the same. The rub wasn't there. The sting was she'd been making do with fantasies and pretending to be happy with the story about being just friends. But being confronted by the knowledge Nick had been seriously involved before had blown apart her pretences. She could no longer deny what she wanted.

What she wanted was Nick.

She'd not only been bitten by the green-eyed monster, she was right this minute being devoured by it.

She wanted to be special to Nick. All she'd had was a kiss on the cheek.

She'd been happy to play it safe. But now it wasn't enough. Now she'd seen evidence that he'd had more than that, but with someone else.

She wanted that someone to be her.

For the first time the mantle of being a responsible aunt and guardian sat heavily around her shoulders. Before, she'd entertained fantasies of going wherever Nick cared to take her, but she'd known they were just that: fantasies. Daydreams she wouldn't actually act on, events she knew wouldn't happen anyway. Now? She didn't begrudge the twins a moment of her time, she'd never regret changing her life to care for them. But she wanted Nick, too. There was no denying it. Fantasies weren't enough to satisfy the desires he'd stirred in her.

Her whole life she'd put everyone else first. Someone asked for help, she was the first to jump. For once, did she dare to not question every damn move she made or, in her case, *didn't* make? Could she go after what she wanted purely because *she* was the one wanting it?

Could she push things between them a little harder or was she only ever going to play life safe?

A fling, that was all, it didn't have to undermine her commitment to the twins. They didn't even have to know! It would all be over soon enough, there wasn't enough of her left to be looking for real involvement.

Safety or desire, fulfilling duty or pursuing what could be an incredible experience?

It all came down to one thing: was she prepared to risk falling flat on her face?

Or wasn't she?

CHAPTER SEVEN

WATCHING the display of emotions flickering across Rosie's face made Nick's heart leap. He was right, the spark of attraction was definitely not one-sided. But why did the timing have to be so lousy?

He'd almost kissed her twice before tonight and each time common sense had stopped him. After the day he'd had he'd probably missed his chance altogether. There were issues at work that had arisen today that needed serious consideration, meaning he couldn't afford distractions, and, as if that wasn't bad enough, seeing Paulo had hit him between the eyes with a stark reminder of Miriam. His involvement with her was the main reason he was now scrabbling to play catch-up with his career and finances. The reason he'd pledged not to get involved with another woman. He had things to do—security, stability, success to build, to recapture.

Then his thigh brushed against Rosie's and he was aware of her right arm resting inches from his. She smelt of roses, just like her name, and she was delectable. And therein lay the dilemma.

Could a kiss be just a kiss?

Could he kiss her and remain steadfast in pursuing his goals?

A kiss wasn't a declaration. It didn't mean he was getting distracted from his mission to rebuild his life, to make it damage-proof.

A kiss couldn't undo all the progress he'd made to rebuild his life. A kiss didn't have that sort of power.

Then he looked sideways right into Rosie's eyes and almost laughed out loud at what he'd been thinking.

Rosie's kisses would have the power to do all sorts of things.

He'd been swayed from his course in life before, badly. He'd promised himself not to let that happen again, under any circumstances. So the fact that Rosie had him thinking about straying from his course was the best evidence that he should steer clear.

For both their sakes.

He'd turned his head and their eyes had met and this time she was certain she'd read his intention correctly. He was about to kiss her. She leant in ever so slightly, prepared to take the risk, prepared for this to be a one-off. She had to know what his lips felt like on hers, how he tasted. A kiss could just be a kiss. She needed it, needed it just for her, wanted something just for her.

And then, ever so slightly, he moved back a little.

The spell was broken and, instead of kissing her, he said the thing she'd have least expected. 'I should explain about Miriam.'

She was at a loss for words.

Truth be told, she'd been dying to know how Miriam fitted into Nick's life since the moment she'd arrived on the scene. But couldn't it wait until he'd actually kissed her? Or was that the problem? Had thoughts of Miriam intervened?

Her frustration and curiosity made her words sound uptight and offended. 'You don't have to, it's none of my business.'

'No, except if things were different, for both of us, I'd be kissing you right now.' He raised one finger and ever so lightly touched her bottom lip. For a brief moment she was in danger of swaying right off the back of the bench, but the touch was over almost the moment he'd made contact. 'But as much as I want to, I can't. My life is complicated right now.'

Rosie swallowed hard, dug her nails into the palm of her hand. 'You think I'd add to the complications?' She had her own reasons why she couldn't get involved but that didn't mean she had to like him having reasons too.

'I know so.' He started to say something else, caught himself and said nothing, sitting tense and silent beside her, knocking the back of his black boot repeatedly against the front of the bench. 'And right now is not a good time. It wouldn't be fair on you.'

'What do you mean?'

'There are things going on that need my full attention. And your life is complicated enough, I don't want to make it more so.'

'Is a kiss really going to be a catastrophe?'

He shrugged. 'Sometimes what we want isn't what we need. Let me explain.'

She didn't want to hear anything except the sound of his mouth on hers. But she nodded. A girl could only ask so many times to be kissed without losing complete pride.

'Miriam walked into my life, or rather I walked into a bar and she was there. Eight weeks later we were married.'

Rosie tried, she really did, but she couldn't help it. She counted the days she'd known him without even a kiss. Miriam had got a proposal from him in only two months.

'She must have been something else.' It was the most charitable comment she could manage under the circumstances.

'She was quite a lot of things, most of all she was very different to anyone I knew. She seemed a free spirit, gorgeous, charismatic. I'm not sure I could have resisted her if I'd tried. I didn't try very hard. It was a case of opposites attract.'

Rosie nodded but couldn't muster one single charitable comment this time.

Nick went on. 'We were both broke but Miriam knew how to have a good time. After the hard slog of years of studying, I wanted a piece of that life. I must have been blinded by her because I thought I'd be able to hang on to the life she offered if we got married.' He laughed but it was a hollow sound. 'Classic tale of the boy from the dairy farm blinded by a girl from the big city. Not that I can pin it on rustic ignorance. I'd been in the city for six years for uni. I'd worked hard and not been distracted, not above the norm at any rate, then I blew it spectacularly.'

'What happened to your marriage?'

'Living like there was no tomorrow took its toll. I kept it up for a while but I couldn't maintain that pace of partying with work. Work won out.'

'Then it was over?'

He sighed. 'Not as quickly as you might think. It was complicated, like these things usually are. But in short I had to work nights and Miriam was out all night having fun. She refused to share any of the responsibilities but was very happy to share my pay packet. Whenever I raised the possibility of her getting a paying job beyond her art, which didn't earn her anything at that stage, she'd accuse me of trying to stifle her creativity.

'Our flat was full of her artist friends so I started sleeping at the hospital. It was the only way I got any rest. We dragged on far longer than we should have and I ended up financing a studio and gallery for her, it was easier than fighting her demands for it. It always ran at a loss. I was too busy to formally call it quits with her and she wasn't about to get rid of me and my salary. I was a consultant by then. We just started living separate lives and eventually I left, with the debts for the gallery a noose around my neck. She had no permanent income so I'd been the financier and had guaranteed the flat to do so.

'I found out later that Miriam had had a string of affairs and, piecing the picture together, I could see they'd mostly been men she thought could help her career, get her showings, introduce her to collectors. Or just lovers to feed her ego. She has no qualms about leaving the ladder of success littered with her cast-offs. She dismisses all her behaviour as a product of creative genius. I was young and naive and I found out the hard way.'

He shrugged. 'I'm over it,' he said as he spread his hands wide, 'but I'm only just emerging from the web of debt. I moved over here to start again and regain my focus on my career. That's what I've been doing. Until now, that's what I've been doing without wavering.'

It told her so much more than the neutral tone in which he was telling her of his marriage, speaking as if he was summarising his work history. 'It's taken me the last couple of years to get clear of that debt so I could start building my practice. The banks wouldn't touch me until then.'

'And what about the other pieces? Other than financial?' She swallowed, shoring up courage. 'If you're over her, why can't you have a relationship?'

There. She'd put it out there. She braced herself almost physically for the rejection she just knew was coming her way.

'For the simple reason I'm not yet in a place where I can commit to one.'

His tone was matter-of-fact and the bluntness of his words were like a punch in her chest.

He continued. 'The only goal I've had for the past three years is to clear the debt and make up for what I lost, not just financially but also time-wise. I'm now, only now, in a position where I can start to build rather than play catch-up. I've sworn I won't get distracted from that. If I do so now, I won't be able to make it up again, the opportunities will pass me by. I can't get involved. I can't give you what you'd need. You or the children.'

She couldn't hear any more, she really couldn't. He'd made his position clear. She and the children weren't going to be a part of his future. 'I've got to go,' she said as she slid down from the bench and made a show of straightening her dress so she didn't have to look at him.

'Rosie…' He stood up from the bench, too, taking a step towards her, but she pretended not to notice and started walking back to the gallery. He fell into step beside her, the distance between them feeling more like a chasm than the metre it was. 'I haven't done a great job of explaining myself tonight. I can't get involved precisely because I can feel the pull between us. I don't think the timing is right for you either. It doesn't sound logical, but that's the way it is. I hope it doesn't affect things between us.'

She stared blankly at him, thinking, What *us*?

'We'll be seeing each other for Charlie's op on Monday. I don't want things to be awkward. For any of us.'

Ah, so that's what he meant. The doctor-patient relationship of *us*. 'Like I said,' she said through gritted teeth, the pain of rejection searing right through her, 'we're both mature adults and I'm sure we can put Charlie's well-being ahead of anything else.'

'That's a given.'

Rosie quickened her step and drew ahead of him.

She wasn't surprised he let her walk away. But she was surprised at how much it hurt.

She drew ahead of Nick and he let her go. It was the right thing to do.

He watched her stride on, her spine stiff and straight, head held high, hair swinging in a golden wave against her back.

His phone vibrated in his pocket and by the time he'd read the text message from James, Rosie had disappeared from view. He wanted desperately to go after her but for what? Chasing her wouldn't solve anything. He'd made his decision. His career had to come first and he couldn't afford to take his eye off the ball again if he wanted to achieve his goals. He couldn't have it all. He'd learnt that lesson once before. He had to let her go.

James was waiting outside the gallery and some of Nick's

black mood settled at the sight of his old friend. Equally tall, James had grown portly where Nick was as lean as in their uni days. Other than that, it could have been any night, years ago in Auckland, and the familiarity was comforting.

'Mate,' said James as he slapped Nick on the back, 'you've got a face like thunder.' He motioned to the gallery behind him. 'Not coming in?'

'I've seen enough. Of Paulo and Miriam's art, at any rate.'

'That bad?' James slapped him on the back again. 'I've seen enough too, it's beer time.'

Ten minutes later they were at a pub on the harbour, nursing a cold pint each, and James had filled Nick in on his latest news.

'Catch me up on you,' he said as he finished. 'How's the practice going? How's your vow of celibacy holding up?'

Nick growled at him. 'There was never any such vow, and you damn well know it. I told you I wasn't going to get involved, not live like a damn monk, and I haven't.'

'All right, take it easy.' James took a sip of his beer before adding, 'So, who is she?'

'Who's who?'

'The chick that's got you all hot and bothered.'

Nick drained the last of his beer and reached for the bowl of chips, grabbing a handful and munching on them, stalling for time before he answered. 'No one's got me hot or bothered. I've got enough on my plate at the moment. I can't afford any distractions, especially with what's happened at work today.'

'What's going on? I thought you'd finally done the impossible these last months and got yourself clear of the gallery and marriage debts?'

Nick nodded. 'Leaving me free to finally start heading in the right direction. I've just bought a house here and simultaneously bought into the practice.'

'Okay, so more debt, but it's the right sort, it's building your career and giving you a place to live. Every self-employed man and his dog have that sort of debt.' James held his beer up to his mate. 'The healthy sort. So what's the problem?'

'One of the partners resigned today, effective immediately, due to ill health. While I understand the situation and he has my sympathy, it means the rest of us have to buy him out. I can't really afford to do that, I'm stretched to the limit with the house and practice debt as it is. If I'd seen this coming, I wouldn't have bought the house. It'll put me back to square one financially. Again.'

He injected the word with all the disappointment he was feeling as he absent-mindedly flicked a chip off the bar table.

'What you're telling me is you're no better off now than when Miriam had finished taking you to the cleaners.'

He shrugged. 'That's how I'm feeling. I know it's a positive thing and necessary to build my practice. But for the first time I was feeling comfortable about the balance, now I'll have to put even more hours into building my practice if I ever want to repay these loans. The reminder of what happened with Miriam plus the partnership issue has poured cold water over the possibility I might have been tempted to get involved with someone.'

'So you *were* thinking about it. Is she hot?' James held out a hand to stall his friend. 'And I don't mean "hot" like Miriam, I mean hot but without the personality of a piranha.'

An image of Rosie's oval face, the bridge of her nose dusted with light freckles, her green eyes sparkling when she laughed, floated into his mind. 'She's complicated.'

'The two of you sound like a match made in heaven. What is it? She married?'

Nick shook his head.

'Divorced?'

Another shake. 'She's the guardian of one of my patients.'

James nodded his head. 'Ah, that sort of complicated. The sort with a kid.'

'Plural.'

'More than one? And you're still keen? Man, this I have to see.'

Nick grabbed another handful of chips and munched his way stonily through his mouthful while James sat chuckling at his expense, apparently enjoying the idea of his predicament immensely.

Nick swallowed. 'Now I know why I don't miss you in all the months between trips.' He met James's eyes, giving in to his urge to laugh in return. 'You're the same pain in the nether regions you always were.'

'And you, my friend...' James lifted his half-empty glass in mock salute '...are in over your head. Here's to the breaking of quite a few vows between now and my next visit.' He gave an exaggerated wink. 'Feel free to text me the details.'

Nick fixed him with a stare. 'There'll be no texting and there'll be no breaking of vows of any sort, even non-existent ones.'

But as they sat and chatted over the next couple of hours, Nick knew the only thing he was certain of was who he'd be dreaming about in the coming nights: the girl with the long limbs and golden hair. The girl who was part of a complicated package that, whichever way he looked at it, didn't gel with the unstable state of his own life.

He couldn't have her and remain in control, keep his life heading in a steady direction.

He couldn't have her and not get involved.

But what would *not* having her mean?

'Charlie, please leave that, we're going to be late.' Rosie pressed her car remote, slung her bag over one shoulder and glanced at her watch. 'In fact, we already are, so *please* come on.'

Charlie turned reproachful eyes up to his crabby aunt from his position crouched next to the car on the ground. He was slowly gathering up the pieces of the intricate Lego model he'd worked on for hours the previous night, and which had slid out of his hands and broken apart as he'd got out of the car.

Rosie, regretting her outburst, stooped down to help him. 'Here, let's pop all the bits in my bag and you can put it together again inside. We'll probably have to wait anyway.' The many bits of plastic now dumped into her bag, she clutched her nephew's hand and they walked quickly to the entrance of the Bondi Paediatric Medical Centre for their appointment with the anaesthetist. She'd just keep her fingers crossed they didn't see Nick while they were in there.

The thought of running into Nick today had kept Rosie awake for the best part of the night. The same thought was behind her impatience with Charlie, which was unfair and made her feel worse than she did already. She'd felt lousy ever since Tuesday night. It was now Thursday, so she just had to get through today, the op and then the follow-up appointment and hopefully she wouldn't have reason to take Charlie back to Nick for a very, very long time.

Never?

Murphy's law was alive and well and they were late for the appointment but they were ushered into Dr Faulding's room for the pre-op visit without sighting Nick. They were in and out in less than ten minutes. It was looking good for getting out of there without bumping into Nick.

She steered Charlie back to the waiting room to pre-pay the anaesthetist's theatre fee.

'Why don't you sit down at that little table over there…' she waved to a low table in the corner of the waiting room '…while I fix up these accounts? See if you can put some of your Lego back together. Okay?'

Charlie nodded enthusiastically and hightailed it for the table, apparently stunned that his aunt was letting him delay his return to school. Rosie handed over her credit card and the various accounts for Charlie's op to the receptionist, watching Charlie absorbed in his work while she waited.

She signed for her bills, wondering if she'd hidden her mood successfully from the twins these last couple of days. With the exception of snapping at Charlie shortly before, she hadn't done a bad job of concealing her distress over Nick.

'Rosie.' She didn't need to turn around this time, she knew that voice. It was the source of her distress, which was why she stalled, folding the receipts and tucking them inside her bag before she turned to face Nick.

And the moment she did, she wished she hadn't. Anger was no match for eyes like his. Anger had no weapons to do battle with her physical reaction to him.

Their eye contact was brief. She looked away, uncomfortable. Spotting Charlie with his Lego, Nick gave a small smile. There wasn't a hint of his amazing grin that always rocked her to her core. Was he hurting too?

'I was hoping to catch you. Have you got a minute?'

Had he been waiting for them? She hesitated; she'd told Charlie he could work on his Lego, so she couldn't drag him out of here now without making a scene. She nodded.

'Can we go to my office?'

'Charlie, do you want to come with me while I talk to Nick or stay here and build?' Charlie pointed to his blocks. 'Okay, I won't be long.'

Nick led the way down the corridor. 'I've been wanting to talk to you but not over the phone.'

Rosie held up her hand to stop him. She couldn't stand the thought he might be about to repeat his words from Tuesday. One night of rejection was more than enough. 'There's no need.'

'There is.' He took her by the arm, his touch gentle, and steered her to a chair while he chose to perch on the edge of the desk, facing her. 'I think we left things on a bad note. I know it sounded like I was rejecting you but I was trying to explain why I couldn't get involved. I'd still like us to be friends.'

She was tired. Tired of beating around the bush, tired of pretending she wanted to be friends. Fatigue made her more forthright than she would normally have been. 'You want to ignore the pink elephant named desire?'

'Something along those lines.'

'We'd be kidding ourselves,' she stated bluntly.

'We're two mature adults, we're both kind of new in town and I wasn't kidding when I said I could use a friend.'

Could she do it? Could she continue to see him, knowing she could only have part of him?

Before she could make a decision there was a hesitant knock on the door and it opened to reveal Charlie. He held the completed model in his hands.

She was glad of the diversion. 'Hi, there, are you finished?'

He nodded as he crossed the room, handing Rosie the model as he leant in close to whisper in her ear, 'Is Nick going to play cricket with me again?'

Rosie looked up open-mouthed, stunned Charlie had spoken to her in front of Nick, albeit in a whisper. Nick's grin and nod told her he recognised the significance of the moment. Charlie went on, 'Can you ask him?'

The little boy tugged at her sleeve again to spur her into action. 'Ah, Nick…' Rosie gathered her thoughts, ignoring Nick's earlier question and focusing on her nephew. 'Charlie would like to know if you can have another game of cricket one day.'

'I can do better than that. If your aunt Rosie is free, we can go and see Australia play New Zealand this weekend.' Standing up, he said to Rosie, 'I've got spare tickets, enough for you and the children.'

Charlie's hand tightened on her arm in his excitement, although he stayed silent. She glanced down to see a huge smile pasted on his face and knew she'd be unable to deny him.

Even so, she was bristling with the feeling she'd been manipu-lated—no doubt Nick had been well meaning but she really didn't have a choice, did she? Charlie was talking in front of Nick. As if this was a breakthrough she'd put at risk. And then she remembered they couldn't make it anyway. 'Saturday we have my dad's birthday—'

Nick interrupted her excuse before she'd finished giving it. 'The game's on Sunday.'

'Sunday?'

At her side, Charlie was nodding. Again she was astounded at his relative comfort in communicating with Nick. If Nick had wanted to get involved, maybe the twins wouldn't have been an issue. Charlie had certainly taken to him. A moot point now, since there was to be no such involvement, no fling. But it looked like they were stuck being friends, at least until the cricket and Charlie's surgery were over.

It would have been better to avoid any more time together before she got more hurt. But Charlie tugged on her hand again and she knew she was caught. She gave in. 'Okay.'

If Charlie's smile was the cake, Nick's was the icing. And that left her feeling very nervous.

She was going to have to play this very carefully if she wanted to emerge from this unscathed.

Sunday arrived eventually and Nick arrived with it, right on time. The twins, who had been had been counting the sleeps before the big day, raced to the front door, bursting with excitement.

If only it was that straightforward for her. She padded down the hallway after them, wondering how she was going to keep up her act of 'just friends' for a whole afternoon when inside she was a turbulent mix of desire and frustration.

She glanced down at her knee-length shorts and plain T-shirt. She'd dressed *not* to impress, hoping it would make playing the role of a friend easier. Method acting for dummies.

She was buddy material and not a woman looking for a relationship. Or even a kiss. Because he'd made it clear and she'd promised herself, *No kisses*.

'Hi, guys, all set?' Nick greeted the twins before turning his attention to Rosie. 'Welcome back. Ready to go?' His eyes gave nothing away. He was being the perfect friend, maybe even a little distracted.

Either way, perfect friends were overrated.

The twins followed Nick out to his car and piled into the back.

Rosie had a flash of what life had been like for her niece and nephew before the accident, their parents in the front seats, kids in the back. Luckily Lucy and Charlie didn't seem to be having any flashbacks at the moment. Rosie had returned safely from Canberra and the twins had been well cared for by their grandparents in her absence. Still, Rosie made an effort to keep the conversation light.

'How did you get tickets for today?' she asked Nick, forcing herself to be the perfect friend, chatty, at ease. In other words, the exact opposite of how she was feeling, which was confused, torn and wanting that evasive kiss, dammit! 'Charlie tells me it has been sold out for ages.'

'A friend of mine is the team doctor for the Kiwis.'

'I'm starting to think you know more people in Sydney than I do. Prime ministers, cricketers…'

'Nah, I only know the people behind the people. Besides, Andrew's only visiting, but the match *is* sold out so it was lucky for us he's here and could get his hands on tickets.'

'What time does it start?' Lucy piped up from the back seat.

'One o'clock.'

'Where are we sitting?'

'We've got seats right on the fence in the members' section so you should be able to get some autographs. If you look in the bag that's on the back seat you'll find some autograph books and pens.'

'What bag?'

Nick glanced around as he waited at a stop sign. 'Damn. I've left it at home. My place is literally around the corner, we'll swing past and pick it up.'

Nick went around the block, turning into a street a few hundred metres from Rosie's. He pulled into the driveway of a large gentleman's bungalow, a solid-looking house, not flashy but it had character. Very much like Nick's car. A huge frangipani tree dominated the front garden. Two old wooden garden chairs sat under its canopy and a swing hung from its branches. The house looked as though it had been well loved once upon a time and now just needed some tender loving care and a new family to give it life. It was much too big for one person.

'Back in a sec.' Nick dashed inside, returning with a large bag, which he handed to Lucy.

'Cool, thanks,' she said. 'Do you think we'll be able to meet the players?'

'Don't be silly, they'll be busy.'

Rosie's eyes nearly popped out of her head when she heard Charlie answer his sister.

He'd *never* spoken out loud to Lucy in front of anyone but close family! Had he forgotten who was driving the car? Whispering to Rosie in front of Nick the other day had been a big milestone, but talking openly! That was something else altogether. Rosie didn't want to draw attention to this event in case Charlie hadn't realised what he'd done. If she made a big deal out of it, it might never happen again. She glanced sideways at Nick, wanting to see if he'd noticed. He inclined his head very slightly, acknowledging the comment.

'But Nick knows the doctor. Do *you* think we can meet the players?' Lucy was still chatting away, to Nick now, also as if nothing astonishing had just occurred.

'I'm not sure, Lucy. We'll have to see when we get there,'

Nick replied. 'If New Zealand do well there'll be more chance, so you'll have to cheer for them.'

'No way,' Lucy said as Nick took the exit for the Sydney Cricket Ground.

Rosie waited, listening, as Nick drove into the car park, but Charlie remained silent.

New Zealand won the toss and chose to bat first. Charlie and Lucy hung their Australian flags on the boundary fence and proceeded to collect autographs from whichever Australian cricketers fielded nearby. They were so busy trying to get the attention of the players they paid no heed to Nick and Rosie.

'Has that ever happened before?' Nick asked, and Rosie knew immediately that he was referring to Charlie's comment in the car.

She shook her head. 'That was a first. He only talks to the five of us—Lucy, Mum, Dad, me and his best friend from school. He will talk to one of us openly in front of the others but he's never talked to us in front of anyone else. The closest he's come was last Thursday, when he whispered to me in front of you.' Nick nodded. 'I thought that was progress but today? That was something totally new. I wonder whether he forgot you were driving.'

'That's possible. Did he chat away when he was little, before he could talk properly?'

Rosie shook her head. 'No, Lucy and Charlie had a made-up language of their own, as a lot of twins do. He used to chat to her, but until they started kindergarten I don't think they spent much time with anyone other than family. Mum used to look after them one day a week when Anna worked and otherwise they were home with her. It was only when they started kindy we really noticed Charlie wouldn't talk to strangers. Lucy chatted enough for both of them. Everyone just thought Charlie was shy, because he talked normally at home by this stage. But by the end of their kindy year, he still wasn't talking to anyone but family. That's when David and Anna took him to a speech pathologist. Eventually he was diagnosed and you know the rest.'

'Maybe today will be the start of a breakthrough.'

'Perhaps the way to encourage him to talk is to introduce people into the family dynamics one at a time so it's not threatening to him.' Afraid that had made it sound like she was propositioning him, she hurried on. 'The speech pathologist suggested that once Charlie is comfortable in a person's company he'll start to ignore them and be able to talk to others in their presence. Eventually that may lead to him being able to talk to new people. Maybe she was right.'

What she wanted him to say was, *Looks like you'd better keep me around then, in order for this experiment to work.*

What he said was, 'It'd be a relief to you. And to Charlie.'

The crowd around them cheered loudly, interrupting their conversation. A wicket had been taken and the New Zealand batsman was making the long, solitary walk back to the pavilion.

Rosie used the break in the match to get her game face back on. Her mask of calm acceptance had slipped a little just then with her disappointment that he was able to keep up the friends act better than she was. Or was it not an act for him? Maybe it wasn't a real stretch to act like she was a buddy simply because that's what she was to him.

She busied herself with the children, reapplying their sunscreen, adjusting hats. All her fussing was unnecessary and Lucy made that obvious when she complained, reminding Rosie they'd had all that done not two hours before. She ignored them and pretended she knew best. Finally, they wriggled from her grasp back to their vantage point at the fence.

'How was your Dad's birthday?' Nick asked when they were alone again.

'Tough, actually. It was the first family celebration since

David and Anna died and their absence was really noticeable.
Dad and Dave had a special bond, which made it even harder.'

'I expect your dad was pleased to have the twins there.'

Rosie nodded. 'The twins were a good distraction except
that Charlie is the spitting image of Dave.'

'Are you thinking of staying in Sydney now to be close to
your parents?'

She shrugged. 'The twins couldn't cope with a move yet but
I've got a bit more time to decide. My work has given me
another month's leave. I've got until the end of the school
holidays now.'

'I can get you a job here if you need it.'

'Thanks, but my boss is prepared to be flexible with my
hours and I need that if I'm the primary carer for the twins. I
guess it's the main factor that makes Canberra an option. It's
a job I can trust and I know I'll be able to manage it.'

'The offer's there if you want it.'

Nick didn't push the topic and Rosie was grateful for that.
She didn't actually feel ready to return to work yet but if pushed
she couldn't have explained why. David and Anna's life insur-
ance payout meant she at least had the finances to allow her
time to make the right decision.

The rest of the day passed in a pleasant blur of hot dogs, ice
cream and easy conversation. When they left the ground at nine
o'clock it was with two very tired but contented children in tow.
Rosie sent the children upstairs to get ready for bed while she
emptied their backpacks.

After being surrounded by a crowd of thousands all day and
having had Lucy chattering away for most of the trip home, the
sudden peace and quiet was a little daunting. Rosie was extremely conscious of Nick standing just inches away from her
as she unpacked the bags.

There was movement in the kitchen doorway. Charlie had
reappeared at the foot of the stairs.

'Can Nick come up to my room? I want to show him something.'

This time Rosie knew Charlie's words were deliberate. Nick was standing at the kitchen bench, in full view, and Charlie was happily talking in front of him and singling him out in his conversation. He still wasn't talking to Nick but this was definitely a step in the right direction.

'Of course,' Rosie said.

Nick followed Charlie up the stairs and paused on the threshold, waiting to give Charlie the chance to change his mind, but Charlie waved him inside. Nick wondered if he would actually talk to him or if they'd be having another one-sided conversation. Not that it mattered, this invitation already indicated an improvement in Charlie's condition.

'Look at this.'

Charlie was standing by his window, looking at the night sky, not looking at Nick.

But he was talking, a huge step for the little boy.

Nick crossed over to him. The house was on the top of a hill and Charlie's upper-floor window had a view across the rooftops to the northern arm of Bondi Beach. Charlie pointed towards the beach. 'Can you see the town hall?'

The town hall and the hotel on the opposite corner were the largest buildings on the esplanade and were both brightly lit and easily distinguishable. 'Sure.'

'Look above the clock tower.' Charlie's eyes were riveted on the view outside. He still hadn't glanced at Nick, but his voice, though quiet, was sure. 'Can you see that bright star up there?'

'I can.'

'That's my dad's star. When Mum and Dad died, Lucy and I saw those stars shooting up to heaven. That smaller star, just next to Dad's, is Mum. They're always together.'

Charlie was whispering now but in the stillness of the room Nick had no difficulty hearing him. 'He can see me when I'm sleeping. He stays awake all night to watch me. I leave my curtains open so that when I wake up during the night I can see him.'

Nick and Charlie stood silently, side by side, watching the star. Nick desperately wanted to gather Charlie up in a big hug but that would encroach on Charlie's carefully guarded personal space. He also knew the hug was more about trying to let Charlie know he understood because he didn't have the right words to express himself. So his only real option was to stand silently beside Charlie, waiting to see what he'd say next, and hope the little boy could feel his support.

Charlie pointed again. 'Look. Dad's blinking.' The starlight was fading in and out, making it look as though the star was winking at them. Nick could hear the pleasure in Charlie's voice.

'So he is. What do you think that means?'

'He does that when he's happy. He's happy now because Lucy and I had such a good day.' And then, Nick saw in his peripheral vision, Charlie glanced at Nick as he spoke. 'Dad likes you.'

'Charlie, that is the nicest thing anyone has said to me in a long time. I'm glad your dad likes me and I'm glad to hear you had a good time today. Should we do it again?'

Charlie nodded his head; he was still looking out the window. 'Yes. Can we go tomorrow?'

'There's no game on tomorrow but as soon as we can, we'll be there. And in the meantime, I'll see you in the morning.' Charlie's tonsillectomy was scheduled for the following day but he didn't spell that out. He resisted the urge to ruffle Charlie's hair and touched him lightly, briefly, on the shoulder instead. 'How about you hop into bed and I'll get Rosie to come and kiss you goodnight?'

If only he was the one who was about to be kissed good-night by Rosie.

But a promise was a promise. And it was as much for Rosie's good as it was for his own. Like he'd thought when he'd first met her, there was a time and a place for everything. And now wasn't theirs.

CHAPTER EIGHT

ROSIE had kissed Lucy goodnight and was standing outside Charlie's room, waiting to tuck him in but not wanting to interrupt. She could scarcely believe what she was hearing: Charlie was not only talking but sharing something so personal with Nick. It was beyond her wildest expectations. He was talking to someone outside the family and, just as wonderful, it was Nick he'd started to trust.

And if that was happening, was it such a stretch to start hoping there was room in her life for Nick? There were only a few small hurdles—she just had to work out exactly what she wanted, get around their promise of friendship and convince Nick he wanted her, too.

She shook her head at the audacity of her daydreaming. Small hurdles! She may as well be standing at the foot of Mount Everest, but, still, maybe she could start imagining what her future might be like. An image of her little family completed by the addition of Nick appeared in her mind's eye and she knew it had been germinating there for some time, she'd just refused to acknowledge it. She'd never before met someone whom she could imagine she might want to have around for ever but she had a strong suspicion Nick might just be it.

She ducked into the bathroom as Nick said goodnight as she didn't want to be caught out listening at the door. Once Nick had gone downstairs she went into Charlie's room but in the few brief minutes that had passed, Charlie had fallen asleep. A shaft of street light fell across his face, which was turned towards the open window and the night sky. Since his parents had died, he'd sucked his thumb in his sleep. Tonight his little hands were clasped together, tucked beneath the curve of his chin, his breathing slow and peaceful, a smile touching the corners of his full lips. The simple image grabbed her by the heart even more than hearing his words to Nick. For the first time since she'd moved here, he was sleeping like a child who was safe. Like a child who had not yet been touched by life's troubles.

The image soothed her heart. She walked over to the window and picked out David and Anna's stars and whispered, 'We're going to be okay.' She'd told herself this before but this time, for the first time, she believed it.

She dropped one last kiss on the tip of Charlie's nose as she left his room then padded downstairs, her heart more carefree than it had been since her brother's death. Even if her scenario of her perfect imaginary family didn't come true, she knew she was finally on the right track with Charlie.

Nick was waiting for her in the kitchen, leaning against the kitchen counter. 'All asleep? Everything okay?'

'Better than okay,' she said, smiling up at him, her eyes alight.

'I take it you heard our conversation?' He came towards her, the smile on his lips reaching his eyes and mirroring her own elation. The effect of his smile was as instantaneous on her as ever, and she smiled back. Nick grinned even more broadly then as he scooped her into his arms and whirled her around. 'Amazing,' he said as he placed her feet back on the floor.

Her hands were still around his neck where she'd wrapped them as a reflex action and they were standing only inches apart, encircled in each other's arms. She tilted her head slightly to look up into Nick's eyes, acutely aware of how close they were, how close their mouths were. Separated by mere inches.

It was so, so tempting to close that gap, to eliminate those few inches. But, amazing as he was, he was also the man who had made it clear he didn't want to get involved. Lifting her mouth to his only to be rebuffed wasn't how she wanted to end the night.

'It's incredible,' she said as she forced herself to let go of him and take a step backwards, concentrating on what was the real breakthrough of the day. 'Do you know how unlikely this was to happen? At his age, to actually be able to overcome his fears to voice his thoughts?' Focusing on Charlie's achievement wasn't made easy by Nick's hands still resting on her forearms. The heat of his fingers marked her skin, tempting her again to overstep the mark they'd set. She swallowed hard. 'It's close to a miracle.'

Nick nodded. 'I've always said cricket was the sport of miracles.'

'Consider me converted.' She made the quip and turned so Nick would have to drop his hands. If he kept touching her, she wouldn't be responsible for what she did. A girl could only take so much and she was learning that promises weren't all they were cut out to be. 'How do I get a season pass?'

'That's football-speak. You've got a way to go before we get you standing at the crease.' He stepped towards her again and her heart flipped in her chest with the hope he was about to break their promise. But all he did was put a hand on her shoulder in a fleeting touch.

'We'll talk more tomorrow but right now I'd better get going. I've got a very important patient on my operating list in the morning.'

It took her a moment to realise he was talking about Charlie's tonsillectomy. It had slipped her mind with tonight's progress.

'I hope he got an early night for his op,' he added, raising an eyebrow at her.

Rosie clutched her forehead and groaned. 'He's going to be exhausted. What sort of an aunt am I?'

Nick laughed as he took her hand and led her from the kitchen towards the front door. 'If you'd had him home and in bed early, the stars wouldn't have been out—'

'And we wouldn't have had our miracle,' she finished off.

They were at the door now and she said a little prayer for the second miracle of the night. A kiss that wasn't on the cheek. A kiss that couldn't be mistaken for one between friends.

Nick pressed his lips for the briefest of moments on her cheek, and a raw sense of longing settled over her. As the door closed behind him, she knew what was behind the longing. She was in deeper than she'd thought.

Somewhere between that first meeting and now, she'd fallen in love with him.

How had this happened? She'd promised to look after the twins, she'd thought her focus was on them, how had she let Nick under her guard? The truth was she'd known she was in trouble from the first moment she'd seen him and she'd just been more in danger with every smile, every glance. When she closed her eyes she could recall everything about him, his smile, which side his cowlick fell to, the little crease he got between his eyebrows when he was thinking and the shape his abdominal muscles made as they tapered into his waist.

She'd fallen in love with him. She'd sell her soul for his kiss. He was the missing piece in this cobbled-together new life she had.

And she'd stupidly, stupidly promised to be just his friend.

Charlie was showing no ill-effects following his surgery. So much so Rosie wondered why she'd spent the night tossing and turning with anxiety over today. Another benefit of parenting, she said to herself: induction into a lifelong acquaintance with anxiety. As she watched her nephew from her seat beside the window, she could see that, far from showing any negative after-effects, he seemed to be lapping up the attention of his sister and grandparents. Maybe the out-of-character behaviour was a further sign of last night's progress?

The private room was perfect, allowing Charlie the freedom to chat to his family without reservations. Rosie had the feeling that Nick had something to do with the room allocation, private rooms would usually be kept for patients who'd undergone more major surgery.

Movement in the doorway made her look up and, as if her thoughts had conjured him up, there he stood. The lazy somersaults she was accustomed to feeling in her stomach when Nick appeared had transformed into crazy loop-the-loops and if she managed to act like everything was normal, it would be astonishing.

She'd definitely fallen for him. Fallen in love, and fallen hard.

He was dressed in a steel-grey suit that emphasised his blue-grey eyes, with a crisp white shirt underneath. He dominated the space but in a confident way, without a hint of arrogance. He wasn't wearing a tie but, other than when Rosie had seen him at the dinner, this was the smartest she'd seen him dressed. He looked fantastic but he also looked as though he was on his way out. Not surprising since it was almost seven in the evening, but she had to bite back regret at the thought of him going somewhere. Without her.

Her parents had turned their heads as he'd entered the room. Nick nodded at them in acknowledgement and then looked at her, clearly wanting her to make the introductions. She stood and gestured from her parents to Nick as she said, 'Mum, Dad, this is Nick Masters, Charlie's ENT specialist. Nick, these are my parents, Jane and Bill Jefferson.'

'Nice to meet you,' he said. He stepped towards them,

smiling, and shook hands with them both before focusing on Charlie. Standing at the foot of Charlie's bed, he flicked through Charlie's case notes, checking his medications. 'How are you feeling, Charlie?'

'My throat feels scratchy.' His voice was raspy.

Rosie felt her parents' startled gazes swivel to her as Charlie spoke, and she nodded at them quickly, confirming she'd explain later.

'Sorry about that. That's what happens when I do my job properly. Now the really important question, did you have to eat any jelly?' Nick grinned at Charlie as they shared their own private joke and Rosie caught her mum's look of appreciation. The full effect of Nick's smile wasn't wasted on her either.

'No.' Charlie shook his head.

'Excellent. Your tonsils came out without any complaints. You'll be feeling as good as new very soon.' Nick reached one hand into the pocket of his suit jacket and pulled out a specimen jar.

'What's that?' Charlie asked.

'These,' he said as he passed the clear plastic container to Charlie, 'are your tonsils. Not everyone has the stomach for it, but I thought you were the type of boy who'd want to see what they look like.'

Charlie inspected the contents of the jar closely. 'Cool.'

'Can I see?' Lucy asked, peering at what looked like two small walnuts in their shells. She gave a dramatic shudder, sticking her tongue out. 'That's gross.'

'Can I keep them?'

'Sure.'

'Sweet,' rasped Charlie, still looking at the jar, oblivious to Nick's apparent enjoyment of the exchange.

'The only question now is, will Rosie mind seeing them on your bookshelf?'

'Nah, she's cool.'

Nick glanced at Rosie, his hands deep in his pockets, his smile not remotely altered. Her laugh was forced. Pretending to be natural with Nick in front of her mum's watchful eyes was not proving easy.

Whereas Nick was as natural as if he'd only met her that morning. Nothing could have been more depressing. Where was the change in expression when he looked at her? Where was the flash of private meaning, a sign of something deeper between them? His expression hadn't changed from the way he'd looked at Charlie. Or her mum and dad.

'Come on, Lucy, I think it's time we went and got you some dinner, if you've still got an appetite after seeing those tonsils,' Jane said to her granddaughter before she leant down to kiss Charlie goodbye. 'We'll see you at home tomorrow, Charlie,' she said, directing an unspoken question at Nick.

'If everything goes according to plan, he'll be home after breakfast.'

Her dad shook Nick's hand as they left the room and her mum bestowed her biggest smile on him. Strange they should meet him and have no idea who he'd become to their daughter. To them, he was just Charlie's miracle-worker, his ENT specialist.

Rosie walked with her parents to the door, telling her mum in a brief whisper she'd explain about Charlie's breakthrough later on.

Nick was checking Charlie's throat. 'How's it looking?' she asked, still trying to act nonchalant and no doubt failing miserably. With her parents gone, it was all she could do to stop from blurting out her realisation of her feelings the previous evening. Nonchalance was too, too much to ask for.

Nick kept his gaze on Charlie. That was probably a godsend. Given her almost total lack of sleep the night before, one slightly sensitive glance would render her a mess. 'Looking good. A touch red but that's to be expected.' He gave Charlie a playful punch in the arm. 'I'll see you in the morning. As long as you've had some solid breakfast like toast and your throat looks okay, you'll be able to go home.'

'Toast? Won't that hurt?' Charlie asked.

'Little bites and drink some juice while you're chewing to soften it, that's the secret. Chewing actually helps your throat muscles. Sometimes your throat can get a bit sorer in a few days, so it might be a bit uncomfortable over the weekend.'

'Can I go to Nippers' training on Sunday?'

'You won't be ready to run around too much by then. You'll need to take it a little bit easy until next week.'

Charlie's face fell and Rosie explained, 'It's just CPR training. They do an annual update, basic first aid and resuscitation practice. No swimming.'

Nick nodded. 'That might be okay. How about we see closer to the time?'

'You could come too if you want, Nick, they always need more helpers.' The eagerness in Charlie's hoarse voice tugged at Rosie's heartstrings.

Nick looked at Rosie, seeming to want her okay. She shrugged as if it was all the same to her. As if!

'The more the merrier.' Him being there would make *her* merry, anyway, but she was doing her best not to let that particular secret out. 'You'd be more than welcome as long as your skills are up to date.'

'I'll see what I can do.' Nick paused as the nurse who was looking after Charlie came into the room, interrupting the conversation. 'I'll let you know.'

All of a sudden Nick seemed in a hurry to leave. It was dark outside now and Rosie's thoughts returned to Nick's plans for the evening. She was conscious of a palpable loneliness, knowing they didn't include her. Nick said his goodbyes, giving Charlie a high-five and reminding the nurse the room was out of bounds to jelly.

Rosie watched him go, mentally crossing her fingers that he'd agree to spend another Sunday with them.

The nurse bustled about, checking Charlie's temperature and taking his other obs. 'Do you want me to organise a trundle bed?' she asked, interrupting Rosie's musings. 'Are you staying the night?'

Rosie brought her attention back to the matter at hand. 'Would you like me to stay?' she asked Charlie.

'I'm okay. I can see the stars from here.'

She hadn't noticed that Charlie's bed faced north-east, the same as his bed at home. He could look out of the window and see the same stars. It was then she knew Nick had definitely had a hand in securing this room for Charlie. Could he get any more perfect?

'Let's get you settled and then I'll leave you to sleep.' She passed Charlie his favourite soft toy, a well-loved dog he'd had since he was a toddler, and put up the bed rail. 'Remember you push this button if you need the nurses in the night,' she said, indicating the call bell that was attached to the rail before kissing him goodnight. 'Sleep tight and I'll be back first thing in the morning.'

Bending down, she kissed the top of his head, smoothing his hair with her fingertips, stroking his cheek. Charlie didn't seem at all anxious about being here by himself. She couldn't believe that would have been the case even a week ago and she knew it was due to Nick.

As she left the room, she was thinking Charlie wasn't the only one Nick had wrought such changes on in such a short space of time. Nick had lifted a good part of the load from her shoulders just by being involved with Charlie's care. Let alone the miracle he'd brought about with her nephew's speech.

And if that wasn't enough, he'd made her fall in love with him. It was a joke, it really was. And the joke was on her because while she was building castles in the sky around the idea of Nick joining their little family unit, he was content with friendship.

She was head over heels. He saw them as 'just friends'. Was there ever a phrase that sounded so warm yet cut so deep?

He knew she was interested in him.

Nick would have been blind not to pick up on that, but so far they were both making good on their promise of friendship. He hoped Rosie would continue it because the thought of having her out of his life did bad things to his head. And at the same time, getting involved was impossible.

Every spare moment he had needed to be spent on building his practice. He couldn't even afford many more lazy Sundays like they'd had yesterday at the cricket. He doubted he'd make Nippers this coming weekend. As fantastic as time on the beach sounded, it was an indulgence he couldn't afford. But, then, how could he not now that Charlie had admitted him into his inner circle? Somehow he'd have to solve this dilemma to everyone's satisfaction. He knew that would be almost impossible.

He was caught.

He'd seen Rosie glance at his attire, knew she'd concluded he was going out for the evening. He wished she was right but instead, he had another meeting with his accountant and he knew that at the end of this, if he wanted to hang on to his partnership, he'd be even deeper in debt.

As expected, he came out of the meeting deeper in debt and even more convinced that a satisfactory resolution with Rosie was impossible. His brief celebration for achieving some of his career and financial goals now looked very premature. And as for every getting involved with anyone, ever again, the idea was ludicrous. Rosie deserved to have someone looking out for her. Not just for her, she was a three-person package deal. She deserved someone who not only adored her but could take care of her. At the moment he was going to be hard-pressed to keep the roof over his *own* head.

He had nothing to offer Rosie's small, vulnerable family.

Nothing but a pile of debt, a banged-up old car and a run-down house with a huge mortgage.

Nick walked beside Rosie, following the twins down the steps to the beach, waiting for her as she stopped on the last step and slipped off her footwear, those ridiculous green flip-flops with the enormous yellow flowers. The rest of her outfit was simple in comparison. A plain white, long-sleeved beach shirt covered most of her, leaving just her long, slim legs on display. Rosie bent down to retrieve her footwear and her shirt rode up higher, exposing a few more inches of tanned thigh. He groaned inwardly.

Why hadn't he just said he had to work when Charlie had reiterated his invitation? It would actually have been more truthful than saying he was free to come. He really wasn't free. There was a mountain of papers he should be attending to right now. On top of which, being around Rosie but unable to act on his attraction was torturous. And they were only twenty minutes into the day.

Was it stress clouding his judgement or was it, purely and simply, Rosie? How else could he explain his presence today? Another Sunday and here he was again, spending the day with Rosie and the children. Why couldn't he stay away?

They made their way to the registration tent erected next to the central lifesaving tower to get their instructions from Douggie, the training coordinator. 'Rosie, can you and Dr Masters run one of the CPR stations?'

'Do we have to teach CPR?' Nick asked, not sure he'd remember enough for that.

Douggie shook his head. 'The paramedics will take the Nippers through the practical first, you just watch them perform

CPR afterwards. There's a list of questions they need to be able to answer, it's pretty straightforward.'

Rosie looked at Nick. 'Sounds good to me,' he said.

'Great. Put these T-shirts on, they'll identify you as being officials so we can see who is supposed to be working with the children.' He handed them each a dark navy T-shirt with 'Bondi SLSC Official' stencilled across the back in large white letters.

'Sure.' Rosie took both shirts and handed him one. In the middle of the tent, without a minute's hesitation, she whipped off her loose white shirt to reveal a white bikini top, a very short pair of shorts and an expanse of smooth, tanned skin.

He was totally unprepared for this scenario *and* for the surge of desire she elicited in him. The intensity of his physical craving for her left him speechless and close to staring.

He wasn't the only one. There was never a shortage of attractive women on Bondi Beach but, even so, a dozen pairs of eyes had swivelled to attention as Rosie slipped her shirt over her head. And now she was standing semi-clad while she shook out the new top. Interested eyes had ample time to appreciate the view.

She had curves in all the right places. Her breasts were perfect spheres, her waist narrow and her hips flared out, giving her a very feminine shape. Her long legs were highlighted by her very short shorts and her stomach was flat and tanned. As she slipped the surf-club shirt on over her bikini Nick wouldn't have been surprised to hear a sigh of regret from the men gathered in the tent.

The thought irritated him. Ludicrous, since she wasn't his, couldn't be his. Frustrated, angry with himself and circumstances, he started to look away but at that exact moment she turned her eyes to him. She'd seen him watching her, and from the smile playing around her lips, the knowledge didn't displease her. Their gazes were locked, their feelings unspoken, yet he knew their thoughts were identical. Rosie smiled, a half-smile, an invitation. She was aware of his reaction.

She picked up a bag of disposable face masks and held them out to him. 'Can you bring these with you?' She paused, running her eyes up and down the length of him as she waited, before adding, 'When you're ready.' She was challenging him. She knew she had the upper hand.

But he couldn't meet her challenge. He had to go on pretending they were friends. Nothing more. For her sake. That was all he could offer. It was that or have her out of his life completely, and that was not an alternative he was prepared to consider.

'I'll meet you at the tent shortly, I'll just have a quick swim to cool off.' They both knew she'd got him all hot and bothered. They both knew it and, tacitly, they both agreed to ignore it.

Nick walked away, pulling off his shirt as he headed for the water. Maybe the cold surf would shock his system into behaving. If nothing else it would buy him some time to recover his composure.

He needed to focus. Focus on his career. And he had enough common sense to know being with Rosie would be a dangerous distraction from his goals.

Work first. Personal life later. Much, much later.

That was the way he'd decided it had to be. And the moment he was tempted to veer from that path was the exact moment he should most doggedly stick to it.

That moment was now.

Thank God the whole resuscitation process was so routine.

Nick was repeating his questions to the Nippers and hearing mostly the same answers in reply. He could almost do this without concentrating, which was a good thing as he was finding it extremely difficult to concentrate on anything since seeing Rosie in her bikini. So much for dogged commitment to his career.

'What are the steps we need to take if someone has collapsed or been pulled from the surf?' he asked as the image of Rosie pulling her T-shirt off over her head came into his mind.

This little boy looked blankly at Nick.

'DR, A, B, C,' Nick prompted.

'Oh, yeah. Danger Response, Airway, Breathing, Circulation.'

'Very good.' Another image of Rosie swam into his head, this time of a toned, tanned abdomen. 'Okay, what danger might we look for?'

'Stingers?'

'Sorry, I didn't catch that?' If the child thought it was because he'd spoken too softly, Nick was happy to let him think that. Only Nick needed to know it was because he'd been sidetracked remembering Rosie's expression when she'd caught him staring at her. She hadn't seemed to mind, she'd looked pleased.

'Stingers and sharks?'

'Yep. Now, show me what you would do to get a response. Show me on the dummy and then we'll do the CPR,' he said as he exchanged face masks on the resuscitation dummy.

He watched as the boy shook the dummy's shoulder, cleared the airway and positioned it ready for CPR, but his mind was on Rosie.

Rosie, who was on the other side of the tent, long legs not remotely concealed by her T-shirt, and apparently not abashed at stealing glances in his direction.

Something had changed between them that morning.

Something it was going to be very, very hard to pretend hadn't happened.

And he had a sinking feeling that something was more than just desire.

He forced his attention back to the children. He'd ignored his needs pretty well over these last few years before he'd met Rosie. He could just damn well go on ignoring them and do what any intelligent, mature man did when his back was up against the wall: refuse to acknowledge anything other than the battle in front of him. Because until he was in a safe place with his work, until he'd proved he was a success, there were no prospects for any lasting happiness.

It was a guy thing. And guys built the castle before finding the girl. That was the way it was, not just for him, for men in general. That was just the way it was.

She'd swear she wasn't the only one stealing glances across the tent. She was sure Nick was watching her, too.

And she knew for certain it had been appreciation in his eyes earlier when she'd changed in front of him. It had been a reflex action on her part. She spent so much time on the beach with the twins she thought nothing of stripping down to her bikini, but she couldn't deny she'd enjoyed having an impact on Nick. She knew she'd been unsuccessful at hiding her own desire for him so it was nice to see that he wasn't completely immune to her.

Thoughts of desire brought back the image of how he'd looked as he'd strode out of the surf after his swim.

Bare-chested and glistening with water, he'd instantly reminded her of the artwork Miriam had made of him. He'd come out of the ocean, shaken the water from his hair and picked up his old T-shirt to rub himself dry. His muscles had rippled and his skin was almost the exact same shade of brown as the wood of Miriam's carving, satiny smooth and shiny.

She'd run her fingers over that carving without knowing it was him, and when she looked at the inspiration for the carving, she'd been hit by an almost overwhelming urge to run her fingers over the real Nick.

Even once he'd slipped the new, dry, surf-club T-shirt over his chest, his muscled torso had still been evident, his forearms still on display. Now she'd seen them in the flesh, her craving to touch him intensified and she was barely managing to stay focused on the task she'd been assigned to.

'Rosie, Rosie! It's our turn next.'

Rosie turned at the sound of her niece's excited voice and saw Lucy and Charlie bounding towards her with their seemingly limitless energy. Charlie's surgery hadn't slowed him down. If anything, it had given him an extra burst of enthusiasm.

'Hi, guys, having fun?' Rosie's heart swelled with love as she looked at her two charges, amazed by the capacity of the human heart to expand to fit all emotions.

The twins sat down side by side on the sand and looked at her expectantly.

'Are you both going to do your CPR with me? What about one of you going to Nick? He's just over there.'

'No, I want you to do it with me, Rosie. We haven't seen you all morning,' Lucy answered.

'Sure. What about you, Charlie?' she asked, but Charlie gave her a silent shake of the head. He obviously wasn't ready to talk to Nick if there was the chance of any other bystanders overhearing a conversation. 'Okay, then. Who wants to go first?'

Lucy volunteered. She was used to being the spokesperson for them both, tackling the challenges and letting Charlie follow in her footsteps. It was ingrained in them both, one to lead, the other to follow, and Rosie hoped, desperately, that one day Charlie would have the confidence to go first. Talking to Nick was a huge step, a step in the right direction, but he obviously was a long way from conquering his mutism for good.

Over an hour later the training session was finally finished but the twins still had limitless energy. The excitement of the morning had left them hyped up and they bounced around Rosie and Nick as they packed the equipment away.

Lucy tugged on her aunt's hand. 'Can Nick come for dinner tonight?'

The question took her by surprise and she wondered if the twins had discussed this at all or if it was solely Lucy's idea. Either way, there was no reason why Nick couldn't join them. 'If he'd like to,' she replied, looking at Nick.

'I'd love to—'

'Yay.'

'But I can't,' finished Nick, not quite meeting Rosie's eyes.

Something didn't fit. He wasn't immune to her, his reaction this morning had left her in no doubt about that, but had he had his fill of them for one day?

'What about tomorrow night, then? We could have a barbecue. We don't have to have salad even, just sausages. They're easy.' Lucy was nodding, trying to convince the two adults.

'Are they indeed?' Rosie laughed as her niece organised their social calendar.

'Lucy, I'd love to but I don't think that'll work.'

Lucy started to pout and Rosie shot her a warning look. 'Lucy, you and Charlie go have one last dip.' Lucy's glance flew from her aunt to Nick and back again before she grabbed Charlie's hand and pulled him down to the water. Inside, Rosie was shrivelling with embarrassment at the thought that Nick was now regretting getting involved with what he must think was her needy family. Maybe she'd totally misread his reaction to her earlier. Maybe it hadn't been admiration in his eyes, perhaps he'd been horrified that she'd so casually changed in front of him. The alternative scenario left her fighting a flush climbing her neck.

'Sorry, Nick, I didn't want you to feel pressured.'

'Rosie, it sounds great but now isn't a good time.' His gaze narrowed, a slight furrow appearing between his eyebrows, one large hand clasped over his forearm in a protective stance. 'There are things going on at work and I really can't afford the time.'

'Everyone has to eat.' The words were out of her mouth before she could think.

'I'd like things to be different but I don't see how that's going to happen.'

Rosie nodded like she understood but she didn't. Not really. 'What if we don't think about how?'

He shook his head and she wondered what she'd been thinking, proposing what she just had. She'd tried it once before at the lighthouse and been rebuffed. When would she learn?

He groaned and rubbed at his jaw. 'It's complicated. Please don't make this harder, Rosie, if you only knew—' He broke off short and hesitated, before saying, 'I can't get involved and we both know a fling won't work, not with the children needing security. Not with you needing security.'

'I'm not looking for a life-long promise of commitment.'

'Maybe not.' He reached out and touched her on the upper arm, his fingers resting there for a moment. 'But it's what you deserve. You and the children.'

'But no one starts a relationship with the agreement they'll be together for ever. Why can't we—?'

'Because I don't know I'll ever be in a position to make that sort of commitment.'

'So because of things that may or may not happen in the future, you won't take a chance on something that's here and now?' she asked softly.

'It can't work.'

Rosie had managed to avoid looking at him but now she looked him right in the eye and said, 'I don't know if you're right about me deserving a life-long commitment and nothing less, but I do know I shouldn't waste more time thinking about someone who has no intention of exploring this attraction we both feel. I'm tired of excuses.' She stooped to collect the twins' bags, slinging their gear over an arm as she straightened up, fixing him with her most defiant glare.

She'd thought she could keep up the act of friendship and that in time Nick would change his mind. But it was costing her too dearly and so far Nick seemed to be getting more adamant that he'd never be anything more than her friend. Friends like that she didn't need.

She adjusted the heavy beach bag and looked at him directly again. 'You're not just a friend to me and I can't go on pretending. Since you won't let go of the charade, I will.'

She turned on her heel and, with as much poise as she could muster when she was walking on soft, hot sand in bare feet, strode towards the sea, where the children were waving to her to join them.

That was her future.

That was all she needed.

And, in time, she'd learn to believe that once again.

CHAPTER NINE

NICK left the final meeting having signed the papers committing him to a bigger share in the medical practice. Having signed the papers committing him to more debt. He was still adjusting to the idea that Rosie was out of his life but at least work gave him something else to focus on.

He stood by his car, trying to work out what to do next. Where to go? It was a Wednesday night and he should be catching up on paperwork or checking his schedule for the rest of the week, but he was too exhausted to think about work.

He should go home but the thought of his empty house wasn't appealing.

His mobile phone rang, distracting him from his thoughts. Pulling it from his pocket, he glanced at the screen 'Home.' This wasn't a call from his home in Bondi. That was still only a house. It could only be one person, in another country.

'Hi, Mum,' he said, confident it wouldn't be his dad. He was a farmer through and through and chatting, especially to a son overseas, was not what he did.

His mum gave him the usual warm preamble but he knew she was building to something. 'Mum, is there something you wanted to ask me?'

He could hear her hesitation. 'I just needed to pick your

brains. Your dad's been having some tests and I wanted to ask you about the results.'

'What sort of tests?' Nick was aware of a tightening in his chest, apprehension making his breath come in shallow bursts.

'He's been complaining for a while that he's short of breath but we just put that down to age and the fact that he's still working the dairy.'

Not once had either of his parents said anything about this symptom and Nick wondered if any of his four siblings knew. 'Is it his heart?'

'Well, we didn't think so but then he had a few chest pains after he'd been doing some fencing and he thought he'd pulled a muscle, but the doctor suggested he get his heart checked.'

Nick wished people who didn't have any medical training would stop self-diagnosing but he figured it would be counter-productive to criticise his mother at this point. 'What's he had done so far?'

'His blood pressure is a little high, nothing too bad apparently, but he had an EKG last week and the cardiologist wants to do an exercise stress test. He didn't really explain what that was all about.'

'Did he mention an echocardiogram as well?'

'I'm not sure.'

'He might have called it an ultrasound,' Nick clarified.

'Yes, I remember that.'

'What they'll do is get an ultrasound picture of Dad's heart while he's resting. It's like the scans Claire had when she was pregnant, checking to see whether the heart's pumping properly and looking at the muscle and valves. Then they'll put Dad on a treadmill and get him to walk so they can see what his heart does when it's under a load. It's just a diagnostic tool but it'll pick up about 85 per cent of cases of heart disease. Who is he seeing?'

'Dr Ahrens.'

'I don't know him but I'll make some enquiries, check him out. Can you get him to ring me when the results come through?'

'Okay.'

'And if you're worried about anything, call me, all right?'

'You're not planning a trip home soon, are you?' He could hear the hope in her voice.

'Not really, things are difficult at work at the moment. But if you really need me there at any time, you know you only have to ask.'

'Honey, one of these days you'll realise life won't stay on hold. Sometimes you have to make room for things, even if they don't fit neatly.'

'What are we talking about now?' Was his mum talking in riddles? 'If it looks like I need to come home when Dad's results come in, I will.'

'It's not just about your dad, it's about your work and you, really. All of it.' There was a pause before she continued. 'When are you going to stop treading water?'

'You mean find a girl, settle down and get married?'

She laughed. 'Yes, that's the general direction I was heading in.'

It was his turn to hesitate, mulling over the question that had been on his mind these last few days. His mum beat him to it.

'You haven't given me your usual reply of, "When it happens, you'll be the first to know". Can I take it from that it *has* happened and I'm not the first to know?'

'Mum, believe me, if I was about to head down the aisle, you'd know it before I did. But, yes, there is someone. And, no, nothing has happened.'

'What's the problem?'

'The timing's wrong, I'm up to my eyeballs in debt and this is not the position I want to be in if I start off with someone new. I want it to be perfect and there's nothing perfect about my life right now.' He looked at his watch. 'Mum, I've got to—'

'Go. Yes, I know, but let me leave you with my piece of wisdom for the day. You don't want to look back over your life one day and realise you lost the girl because you were waiting for everything to be perfect. Don't make excuses because you're afraid to take the risk of loving again. Life isn't perfect, so if you're waiting for the perfect moment, I can tell you, it's not coming.'

'I kind of guessed that. Look, I'll ring you in the next few days but call me if something comes up with Dad or you're worried for any reason.' He ended the call and thought about his mother's words.

Was his mum right?

Was he making a mistake waiting for the perfect moment?

He didn't know. He just didn't know.

His recalled his mum's accusations that he was making excuses for not getting involved. Rosie had virtually accused him of the same thing. They'd both been right: he'd given Rosie every excuse why they couldn't be together and he'd been so damn pigheaded he hadn't considered whether there might be some very good reasons why he should ignore every single one of those excuses.

Was he making a mistake, assuming he knew what Rosie needed?

Finally, his mind cleared and the solution seemed simple.

He unlocked his car and slid behind the steering-wheel. 'Friends be damned,' he said as the engine sputtered to life and he pulled out of the car park, certain about *what* he was going to do, just not that sure about *how*. 'Details,' he muttered as he pulled out into the street. 'Details are overrated.'

'Lucy,' called Rosie, 'can you grab me a plate for the hamburgers please?'

Lucy raced into the kitchen, yelling for Charlie, who was somewhere inside. 'Charlie, dinnertime. Come and get it.'

Rosie shook her head at her boisterous niece and turned back to the barbecue. She was flipping the burgers when Lucy returned so she held her hand out for the plate without fully turning around.

'Thanks, honey,' she said.

'Any time, sugar.'

At the sound of Nick's voice, she jumped, startled, dropping the barbecue tongs and registering vaguely that they clattered to the ground. 'I thought you were Lucy!' She'd turned around now and saw she hadn't imagined him. Nick was here, in a dark suit and white shirt, open at the neck, his tie missing. He looked tired, dark shadows under his eyes.

'I bribed them both with a couple of Perky Nanas so I could bring the plate out. There's a business model in there somewhere: behaviour management courtesy of New Zealand confectionery.'

'I think…' she smiled despite being both bewildered he was there and trying vainly to hold on to her anger '…that's already patented under bribery.' She glanced down at the plate he'd handed to her and, remembering what she'd been about to do, turned back to the barbecue to pile the burgers on to it. She was aiming for cool and calm and probably coming across as crazy, but what was a girl to do? 'I wasn't expecting you,' she said, brave enough to say it now her back was turned. She kept her voice level and it was the most neutral thing she could think of to say but still get her point across. She thought she was doing a good job, all things considered.

'I know I said I couldn't come…'

'Not just for a barbecue. You said never.'

'And I thought I meant it.'

She'd finished with the burgers and she turned the barbecue off, having no more reason to delay. She turned to face him.

'I thought I meant it,' he repeated, 'but I realise I've never meant anything less.'

Her legs suddenly shaky, she slid the plate back onto the barbecue, unsure what she was about to hear. He was looking at her intently, his features serious. He looked exhausted, she realised, not just tired. What exactly had been going on?

He shoved a hand through his hair and flicked a gaze over her face, settling on her mouth before raising his eyes to meet hers.

'Will you hear me out?'

Rosie hesitated, then nodded. Who was she kidding? Nick being here was as much of a miracle as Charlie talking to Nick had been. Staying angry just to prove a point would only prove she was a numbskull when it sounded like he might have had a change of heart.

She nodded and he looked relieved, like he'd doubted his reception.

'It's been a helluva few days, Rosie, heck, if I'm honest, it's been a helluva few weeks since I met you. I feel like I've been on a roller-coaster. I haven't known which way is up. I've had unexpected dramas at work that have needed all my concentration but I've found that so difficult because I'd met you. I want to spend time with you, and the children, I'm drawn to you in a way I can't explain, but I've tried to keep my distance.'

'Why?'

'Because I told myself I couldn't afford distractions. After my divorce I reaffirmed my old goals I'd strayed so far from, and when I met you I was well on my way to achieving those. I'd bought into the practice partnership and I was finally feeling stable, confident of where I was heading, but then the night I ran into you at the art gallery there was an unexpected hiccup. One of the senior partners made a sudden decision to retire, which put me under the pump financially. I told myself I had to sort that out before I could move forward. That'll take years, in financial terms. Until I had that under control I had nothing to offer anyone.'

'And now?'

'The situation itself is resolved, we've bought him out, but I'm now further from my goals. The big realisation for me was that, because of that situation, I was making assumptions and decisions about you and for you that I have no right to make.'

'Like this "just friends" idea?'

'Yeah.' He grinned and the lines of fatigue around his eyes fell away. 'Like that. I don't want to be the sort of person who thinks they know what's best for someone else.' He stepped closer, reaching for her, his hands resting lightly around her upper arms. 'I tried hard to convince myself that you were just a friend because it was safer, because I didn't think I had anything to offer.'

'You didn't need to offer me anything, I only wanted you.'

'It's never that simple.' He traced a line down her arm, from her shoulder to her wrist, which he circled with his fingers, leaving her shivering for more. 'It still isn't, not for me. But I admit it, I can't control everything. Even though my timing isn't perfect, my life isn't perfect, I want to be a part of your life. And not as "just friends". I need to know—is there room in your life for me? You've got two children who need stability, two children who need your attention, so I'll understand if it can't happen, if there's only room for a night or two. You need to make that decision, I see that now. It's not mine to make on your behalf.'

He slid his fingers from her wrist to take her hand in his. 'That's a long way of saying I'm falling for you, Rosie.' His gaze caressed her face, lingering on her lips before coming to rest on her eyes again. 'I'm hoping you feel the same.'

She nodded, scarcely daring to breathe in case the moment vanished as magically as it had appeared.

'We'll have to take it slowly. And while I'm not sure where we're headed, I do know the direction I want to head in is with you.'

She nodded, eyes wide. 'I hoped for a time that you cared

for me but I couldn't be sure and then you seemed so set on being friends only…'

'An idea destined for failure.' He brought his other hand up until he was cupping her face. He lowered his head and it was an automatic reaction for her to lift her mouth to meet his. As her eyes fluttered closed, she knew this was right. She felt his breath on her lips and waited for the touch of his mouth.

The squeak of the back door interrupted the moment and she knew their solitude was over. As the twins burst out onto the deck Nick dropped his hands and Rosie stepped back, smacking against the barbecue. They must have looked as guilty as a couple of teenagers caught out kissing in the classroom.

'Rosie, we're starving!' The twins slid to a halt, flanking Nick on each side, appearing oblivious to their aunt's flustered state.

'Hi, Nick,' Lucy said, as calmly as if he dropped by for dinner every day.

Charlie peeked around Rosie and saw she'd finished cooking. He picked up the plate piled with hamburgers and carried it to the table as Lucy took Nick by the hand, saying, 'You're a few days late but I knew you'd come.'

Rosie wished she'd had her niece's confidence. It would have saved her three sleepless nights since Sunday.

Dinner was relaxed, the conversation bouncing backwards and forwards between all of them. There was no chance for her and Nick to have any sort of adult conversation but the interaction between them all was natural and fun. From what she could tell, Nick was enjoying himself too. But conversation was not where her mind kept drifting. How could she concentrate when he'd been about to kiss her?

At the end of dinner the twins cleared the table, depositing the plates in the kitchen before disappearing, as they always did, to do some last-minute things in an effort to delay their bedtime. Rosie managed to catch them to make them say goodnight to Nick, knowing they'd save that as an excuse to come back downstairs again.

Lucy hurled herself into Nick's arms, hugging him tight and giving him a noisy kiss on the cheek before rushing over to Rosie and giving her similar treatment. There were no half-measures with Lucy.

Charlie was a different matter. He approached more quietly after his sister and looked solemnly at Nick, almost eye to eye as Nick was still sitting down, standing for a moment as if considering something. Then he seemed to make his mind up and, stepping forward quickly, he leant in to give Nick a quick hug. He whispered something in his ear before turning and bolting up the stairs after his sister.

'What did he say?' There was no way she was playing coy on this one.

'He told me I'm not just his doctor, I'm his friend too.'

Rosie's hand fluttered to her chest. 'Really?' She sat down, hard, on a chair while she thought this over. Watching the children interact with him, she thought how well he suited having kids around. Maybe a slow and steady approach could get them over the finish line?

If she didn't rush things and if the children had time to get used to the idea, maybe there could be a future for her and Nick. And maybe the same approach would work for Nick too, slow and steady? He was here after all. If he got used to them as a family perhaps he'd find it hard to give them up.

Fixing Nick with a look, she said, 'You are something else, Nick Masters.'

He tipped an imaginary cap at her. 'I'm glad to hear it, because I came tonight knowing it was most likely I'd blown my chances with you. Which I think is where we were at in our conversation when the twins came bursting through the door.'

Rosie shook her head, stood up and walked around the table to him, her heart rate rising, cheeks flushed. He hadn't taken his eyes off her and the desire she saw in his face soothed her nerves. Drawing courage from the pent-up desire she'd been burdened with these last weeks, she slid onto his lap. He drew in a sharp breath and she smiled, lowering her head close to his, picking up his hands and placing them on either side of her face.

'I think,' she said, hearing her breathing quicken, 'this is where we were.'

There were no words spoken between them. They both knew what would happen next.

This moment had been coming for a while. It was inevitable and she needed to feel the touch of his lips, to taste him, savour him.

She licked her lips and Nick groaned, pulling her tight against his chest and tipping her face down to his. The moment his lips touched hers, Rosie was no longer quite aware of where she was—all she knew was this moment should go on for ever. She was no longer sure where his body ended and hers started, couldn't have said whether she was standing or sitting. There was only the kiss. Nothing else. Only Nick's mouth on hers, touching, kissing, caressing, as if they were made for this moment. She sank deeper into his touch, his taste, all her senses trained on Nick and how he was making her feel. Every molecule was alive with his touch and her head was pounding with desire.

He ran a hand from her cheek to her shoulder and down her arm to her elbow, leaving a trail of fire in his wake. Then, slowly, gently, he ran his fingers under her T-shirt, touching the sensitive skin at her waist. Rosie had to bite her lip, afraid she would moan out loud.

He rested the palm of his hand against her ribs and she could feel the beat of her heart, pulsing under his fingertips.

She parted her lips as gentleness was replaced by hunger and wanton desire replaced all pretence of friendship as they explored and tasted each other, immersed in the moment.

The screaming penetrated the bubble of sensation they were enclosed in. Rosie sprang back from Nick and onto her feet as if boiling water had been flung over her. She was disoriented and it took a moment for reality to come clear, a moment before she registered the scream was Charlie's.

He was standing right next to them. Neither had heard him come back downstairs. His chest was heaving, his eyes bright with angry tears.

'What are you doing?' His voice was a raspy growl, like nothing she'd ever heard from him. She'd never even seen him mildly angry and now he was almost beside himself, and it was terrifying. He wasn't looking at Nick, didn't even seem to see him there, but he stared at Rosie without blinking, his hands balled into fists at his sides.

For a moment she thought he was going to strike out at her and she took a step closer to him, but he moved back and at that moment, Lucy appeared in the doorway, her gaze moving over the scene. She seemed to know exactly what had happened. Without speaking, she ran to Charlie's side, looping her arm about his shaking shoulders, and at her touch, Charlie seemed to collapse, all the anger whooshing from him as if he were a burst balloon. Lucy fixed Rosie with a stare that labelled her a traitor and, turning her brother around, she held him tight as they headed for the stairs.

Neither of them looked at her again. Then they were gone.

Rosie collapsed onto an empty chair, her hand fluttering to her throat where there was a constriction so tight she vaguely wondered if she might stop breathing. She couldn't take her eyes off the empty doorway.

'What have I done?' She grasped her throat tighter and continued to stare after the children as if she might magically conjure them up again. And all she could whisper, over and over, was, 'What have I done?'

* * *

The moment had transformed from pure beauty to sheer horror in a matter of seconds. Nick wasn't sure he'd even processed it yet. But he knew he was responsible for deeply upsetting a little boy he was supposed to help. He was his *doctor*, for Pete's sake.

He wasn't sure what had happened—he cut the excuse off. He knew *exactly* what had happened. He'd been kissing Rosie. The woman his mother had, in the few short minutes of a single phone call, managed to work out was 'the one'. Even before he'd worked it out.

And he, idiot that he was, had been so caught up in the incredible realisation he was kissing the woman *he was in love with*, he'd paid no heed to anything else.

What a time to be hit over the head by the knowledge he'd fallen in love.

And now they would pay. Worse, it seemed the children would pay for their recklessness, his and Rosie's.

He couldn't let that happen. He had to fix it.

'Rosie.' He bent over her chair, touching her shoulder, not sure if she was still aware of his presence. 'I'll go after them.'

'No!' So she'd heard him. And her rejection was decisive. 'No,' she repeated, '*I* have to go.' She stood and held herself rigid, her face pale beneath its smattering of freckles. 'I can't believe I've done this to them. I forgot. For a moment, I forgot. About everything except myself. Myself…' she turned anguished eyes to him '…and you.' And then she repeated, as though to herself, 'What have I done?'

The part of him that needed to fix things couldn't stand it. He pulled her to her feet, held her firmly in front of him and ducked and moved until his face was directly in her line of vision and she had to look at him. 'Rosie, don't look away. Look at me.' He waited until she complied. 'You've done nothing wrong. Our timing could have been better but we've done nothing we can't fix. Do you hear me?'

Rosie was listening now. He could see he had her attention. Now he just had to say something that got through to her. He *had* to fix this. 'Charlie's upset, that's all. He's had a lot to deal with and it all came out in his reaction just now. He wasn't reacting to you and me, he was reacting to the stress of everything that's happened to him.'

'We don't know that.'

'But it makes sense,' he said, trying to convince her, convince them both.

She nodded. She looked like she'd heard what he'd said and at least she hadn't told him not to be ridiculous.

'You go to them now. I'll stay here if you want or I'll go. But if I go, I'm only a phone call away and you ring me.' He tilted her head up so she had to meet his eyes. 'It doesn't matter what time it is, you ring me and I'll be here.'

A glimmer of a smile crossed her lips. 'Thanks, but don't stay. I think this is something I'd best do alone. Even if Charlie wasn't just responding to you and me, we're still part of the problem.'

'Which part?'

'I'm not sure, but he looked at me like I'd betrayed him.' There was more she wasn't saying but he knew instinctively now wasn't the time, that she wouldn't say anything else until she'd seen the twins.

Gathering her in his arms, he wrapped her in a hug and she dropped her head to his shoulder and clung to him as though it was the last time.

Did it all end here tonight?

He didn't really think that would happen, but the way Rosie was holding him tight, as if she was memorising the fit of her body to his, he had a sinking feeling that was exactly what was on her mind.

When she eased out of his embrace, she ran her fingers down his face, trailing a fingertip over his lips, slowly, caressing. She looked sad, and stressed, but the far-away look in her eyes also told him her mind was now with the twins.

'I'll speak to you later,' she said, and held his hand for a brief moment before turning and going inside.

A conversation was playing in his mind as a backing track to Rosie's departure. His mum had told him he'd look back over his life and realise he'd lost the girl because he'd been waiting for everything to be perfect. Had he waited too long? And when he'd finally acted, had he failed to think it through and do it properly?

From where he stood, it seemed like that might be exactly what had just happened. And that losing the girl he'd fallen in love with was the price he'd pay.

But he'd be willing to bet even his mum wouldn't have thought it would happen this quickly.

Rosie stopped mid-tread at the top of the stair as she heard the front door close. Nick had gone. She finished climbing the stairs. Lucy's door was open but her room was empty. Charlie's door was shut. She knocked several times before the handle turned and she was begrudgingly admitted by a stony-faced Lucy. Charlie was on his bed, his back turned to her, and she couldn't tell if he was asleep or not.

She reached out to take Lucy's hand and Lucy stepped back, unimpressed. She walked into the room and sat down on the chair at Charlie's desk. Lucy sat on the bed next to Charlie, one hand resting on her brother's back.

'Lucy, can you tell me what's wrong? Why are you both so upset?'

'You were kissing Nick.'

'Yes.'

'Why?'

'I like him. He's my friend. He's your friend, too.'

Lucy shook her head and Rosie saw Charlie shake his head, too. He wasn't asleep.

'He was only pretending to be our friend but if he was our friend, he wouldn't kiss you.'

Charlie still wouldn't look at her but at least Lucy was talking.

'He can be our friend, all of us,' Rosie tried.

'No,' said Lucy. Her chin was tilted in a way that spelled trouble. Lucy could be stubborn when she got her mind set on something. It looked like she'd set her mind on Nick and Rosie. 'He'll want you, not us. Mummy and Daddy went away on a trip and they didn't come back. Mummy and Daddy kissed like you and Nick. That's what grown-ups do when they kiss. They go away on holidays and *they don't come back*.' Lucy's vehement words ended on a gulp but, true to her resolute nature, she didn't let the tears gathering in her eyes spill.

The room seemed to go hazy and Rosie blinked to pull it back into focus. If she hadn't known it was impossible, she'd have sworn her heart had just been snap-frozen and cleaved in two at the picture of fear and loss Lucy had just painted.

What have I done? She knew she'd be asking herself that same question over and over. Not only had she managed to let the twins down by failing to ease them into the new situation with Nick, she'd managed to revive, and magnify, their fears that they'd lose her, too. Just like they'd lost their mum and dad only a few short months ago.

'Lucy…' Rosie stood and crossed over to Lucy but her niece shrank back as if she were a stranger.

'We've got each other. Charlie and me. That's all we need.' The look on Lucy's face made Rosie's blood run cold.

'Nothing will ever make me leave you, Lucy.'

Lucy turned her head away and lay down next to her brother, holding him tight. As she did, Rosie heard her say, her voice raspy with tears, 'We don't believe you.'

Rosie stood and watched them, her hand back at her throat,

wondering how she'd managed to destroy the love the twins had always had for her. The love and the trust.

In the haze that had descended on her life tonight, there was only one thing clear: until she earned the twins' trust again there was no future for her with any man.

And especially not with the man she wanted. The man who she'd only just found out had feelings for her, too. Now would she ever find out just how deep those feelings ran or where they might end up?

Rosie felt sick.

She had, in fact, felt sick almost every second of the last two days. She'd picked Charlie up early from school for his Friday afternoon appointment with Nick. The moment she'd seen him heading for her car, the ball of stress sitting at the base of her throat had tightened a little more.

It would have been easier to manage if the twins had railed and ranted at her. If they'd been slamming doors, it would have been a breeze. But since Wednesday night in the bedroom, Lucy had only spoken to her when strictly necessary and had not made direct eye contact. Charlie had neither spoken to nor looked at her. Not once.

Rosie put the radio on as they drove to the medical centre, hoping to mask the uncomfortable silence. While she drove, she thought about the last few days. She'd spoken to Nick briefly when the twins had been at school. She didn't dare risk a conversation when they were at home. She'd gone over and over the situation with her mum. She'd had a phone call with Charlie's psychologist, who was interstate and couldn't see Charlie until she was back in five days. Until then, the best any of them could come up with was to give the children time and keep reassuring them.

And unless there was a miracle with Charlie today when he saw Nick, she'd decided what she had to do.

She had to give him up.

They'd only been in the waiting room for a matter of minutes when Nick, looking as pale and tired as she knew she was, came out to call them into his office for Charlie's review. The knot of tension in her throat intensified. Although she wanted this over, she also wanted to delay it for as long as possible. She was sure the outcome was not going to be the one she wanted.

'Charlie, Rosie, you can come through?'

Rosie manoeuvred herself so that Charlie had to go ahead of her. Nick was waiting in the corridor, facing them, and over the top of Charlie's head she could see the silent query in his expression. She shook her head in answer. Not good.

It didn't improve. All the questions he directed at Charlie were met with stony silence. Charlie complied with Nick's brief physical examination but he might have been a doll, he was so passive.

On their way out, Nick said softly to Rosie, 'Call me tonight.'

Rosie nodded as she fleetingly met his gaze. After tonight there'd be no need for any out-of-hours phone calls. The only times they'd be talking would be at Charlie's appointments. She supposed she should even change Charlie to another specialist.

She should never have veered from her path of responsible aunt.

After tonight, she and Nick would be over.

And the way it was hurting already, she wished it had never even begun.

'Why are we whispering?' Nick had started the conversation off at normal volume but his voice had now dropped down to Rosie's volume.

'I don't want the twins to wake up.' Rosie was sitting up in bed, hunched under her covers with her knees drawn up to her chest, whispering into the receiver like a schoolgirl not wanting her parents to hear.

'It's eleven o'clock at night!'

Rosie knew that. She'd watched every minute tick past on the clock as she'd delayed time and again in ringing Nick. She'd tried to delay the inevitable but the moment was upon her.

'We can't see each other.' She blurted it out, her voice rising above a whisper. She had to get it over with, the torment of ending it with the only man she knew now she'd ever really loved.

'It just needs time—'

'No, Nick, I don't think so. It's not like the twins are just being headstrong. They are seriously affected. I don't think I even know the extent of what I've done yet—'

'Rosie, stop right there.' He was no longer whispering, he was angry and not trying to hide it. 'You've said this sort of thing too many times these last couple of days. There is one thing you have to get through your head: you've done nothing wrong. We could have handled it better, sure, but we can only say that with hindsight. You're acting like you're guilty of…' He paused. 'That's it. That's what you're doing.'

He hurried on, and she knew he'd worked out exactly what she was torturing herself with. 'I told you once I thought you've always taken care of others, put everyone's needs first. And that's what this is about—you're eaten up with guilt because you gave some credence to your own needs. You think what's happened is divine punishment for your selfishness.' There was a long silence and then he spoke again. 'Tell me I'm wrong.'

She couldn't. It was exactly what she thought but even hearing him say it out loud did nothing to dent that belief. If anything, she believed it all the more for hearing someone else say it.

'That's part of it, Nick. It doesn't really matter because, however I feel about it, the fact is there are two children who've recently suffered a double bereavement which you and I can't begin to fathom. And now they're reliving their loss, they're terrified the same thing will happen to me.'

'Why aren't they talking to you, if they're so worried about losing you?'

'I think it's because they don't trust me, they're trying to protect themselves and they're angry at me. It's all muddled up with their anger at their mum and dad for leaving them. They think *I'm* going to leave them, like their parents did.'

'They think you'd *intentionally* leave them?'

'I don't think it's that. I think in their minds that if you and I got together, we'd go away and we wouldn't come back. They don't distinguish between deliberate actions or otherwise. They don't understand intent. They don't understand their mum and dad didn't want to leave them.'

'But we won't leave them!' Nick was roaring now, and Rosie knew it was because he was no longer able to contain his frustration at the events he couldn't influence. 'I'm not going anywhere. Damn it, I'm in love with you, Rosie.'

'You are?' Rosie breathed it into the phone. She'd had no idea his feelings ran that deep. Oh, she'd hoped and dreamed but she hadn't known. But to find out now, when she knew she couldn't have him, was too cruel.

'I am, and I want the whole deal.' She could hear the conviction in his voice. 'Now you're telling me it's over?'

'What else can I do?' Her cry was full of the anguish in her heart.

'I don't know, Rosie, and it kills me that I don't. But you can't give up on us. You can't. I love you. That's all there is to it.'

Just like with the twins, if he'd yelled and screamed at her, it would have made it easier to bear. But where he'd momentarily raised his voice a few moments ago, now it was steady and firm.

'I don't know what else to do. I can't make promises to you I don't know if I can keep. I know you understand, you told me the same thing. I promised the twins I'd look after them, that I wasn't going anywhere. Now they think I can't be trusted. If I have to spend the next ten years putting this right and making them feel secure, I will. Whatever the cost.'

'Then there's nothing left for me to say.' Nick spoke quietly. She could detect neither sadness nor anger in his voice. She didn't know what to make of it and she guessed she'd never know.

He hung up first, the sound of the receiver being replaced signalling the exact moment her heart broke.

It was over.

She'd lost everything.

CHAPTER TEN

FOR the fifth time that week Nick left the office after dark. His days had been unbelievably long; he'd been at work before sunrise most days as well. Keeping busy, trying to keep his mind off Rosie and the children. He was exhausted. He'd had enough of the office but mostly enough of the mess his life had become. Amazing what could happen in the space of a single week, he thought. In less than seven days he'd lost the only woman he'd ever truly loved, doubled his already crippling business loan and helped traumatise two small children who now detested him.

And, sadly, he added to the inventory as he left the building, my new best friend in Sydney, other than my business partners who are as impoverished as me, is my bank manager. And he only loves me for my debt.

He shoved a hand through his hair, thinking absent-mindedly that he really should get it cut but knowing he wouldn't get around to it any time soon. What did it matter?

He got into his car, turning his mobile phone on and plugging it in to recharge. It rang almost immediately.

'Nick!'

'Mum, what is it? Is Dad all right?' He barked his words out of anxiety.

'Dad's fine, but are you okay? You don't sound like yourself.'

'I've never felt less like myself.' He switched the car engine off, leaving the power on to charge his phone while he filled his mum in on the events of the last ten days, the concise version. 'You can say you told me so. You warned me I'd lose her,' he said as he finished the summary.

'I'd never say I told you so but why didn't you tell me any of this when I rang to tell you Dad's results the other day?'

'I was hoping I'd wake up and find it was all a bad dream.'

'And now what?'

'Now it's over.'

There was a pained silence from the other end. Then his mum said, 'Australia must have done something to you, because the son I raised would never give up on his girl.' She sighed, the sound conveying her exasperation better than any words. 'Your whole life, Nicholas John Masters, I've never known you to be a quitter. Ever. Not even when you maybe should have been.'

'You also raised me to believe no means no.' It was the first time he'd smiled properly all week. 'Get your messages straight, Mum.'

She tut-tutted at him. 'Don't give me your clever doctor-talk. There's only one thing you have to do. I'll be waiting to hear from you when you figure out what that is.'

'You're going to keep me in suspense?'

She sniffed, pretending offence. 'I'm not the sort of mother who interferes in her son's relationships. But just so you know, there'll be four places set at Christmas lunch if you feel like surprising us.' She blew him a kiss down the line and ended the call, obviously wanting to have the last word.

He thumped his head back on the headrest, mulling over the quandary he was in.

A series of the most familiar sayings his mum had raised them on rang in his ears. Growing up, she'd seemed to have one ready for each and every occasion that had presented itself. For every problem, there's a solution; we are not a family of quitters; you only find out who you really are when your back's against the wall; never turn away from someone in need.

The thing about clichés, he reflected, was that they became clichés because they're based in truth. Somewhere in those trite expressions, he'd find the blueprint for what he was meant to do.

It didn't take long.

He hadn't been raised a quitter.

But he'd been so focused on respecting Rosie's decision that they were over, he'd failed to consider what was actually best for Rosie, for all of them. And he could see now they weren't always the same thing.

He lifted his head, turned the car back on and drove out onto the street.

The time for inaction was over.

The time to get his girl was now.

Philip had arrived on their doorstep just as he and Lucy were finishing dinner. Auntie Rosie had let him in. Philip had even tried to be friendly but Charlie knew he wasn't interested in either him or Lucy. That was one of the best things about not talking to people—it meant he could watch them, work them out. And what he'd worked out pretty quickly was Philip really wanted to talk to Rosie by herself. He also knew Philip didn't really have the first clue what to say to him. That suited Charlie just fine; there was nothing he wanted to say to Philip, either.

What he did want was for everything to go back the way it had been. With his mum and dad. And if he couldn't have that then he wanted Auntie Rosie to stay with them for ever. What he didn't want, what he wouldn't take, was being left again.

Without needing to discuss it, he and Lucy had gobbled their dinner as fast as they could, refused seconds and fled upstairs. He'd pretended to be reading in bed but once Rosie had been up to check on them, he got out of bed and was now perched at the top of the stairs, holding on to the rails out of sight but within earshot of the grown-ups. He could usually hear most of what was being discussed in the kitchen if he sat here, something he'd learnt ages ago, when his mum and dad had still been alive.

Right now, he didn't like the direction the conversation was heading.

He crept into his sister's room. 'Luce,' he whispered, 'come.' He placed a finger against his lips to show her she had to be quiet.

'Why?'

'Come on, you have to listen. They're talking about moving to Canberra.'

'Who is?'

'Rosie and Philip. Philip wants Rosie back there.'

'What about us?'

'I don't know, that's why we have to listen. Hurry.'

Lucy jumped out of bed and the two of them tiptoed to the top of the stairs.

They could hear Rosie say, 'Didn't want children?'

'Let's not go through that again. It'll be a fresh start for us.'

Rosie was sighing. 'How on earth do you think this would work?'

'Simple. You move back to Canberra, you can work part-time and we see how things go. Of course, the apartment isn't big enough for the children—'

Lucy turned frightened eyes on her brother, who reached out to tuck her hand in his, but their movements caused the floor-boards to creak. They froze, and the conversation downstairs stopped.

'Come into the sitting room,' they heard Rosie say. 'We can't talk here.'

The twins curled up further out of sight at the top of the stairs, listening as the adults went into the front sitting room and closed the door.

'They're going to leave us behind?' There were tears in Lucy's voice and Charlie burned with the anger that never seemed too far away these days. They couldn't do this to them! They couldn't.

'That's not going to happen, not ever.' Charlie didn't recognise his own voice. He'd thought his voice would wobble but he sounded so certain. He knew he must be scared but he couldn't feel it, he couldn't feel anything. He'd fix this. He'd fix it properly, he thought, as an idea surfaced.

He whispered his plan into Lucy's ear and her eyes widened but she nodded. They crept to their rooms before meeting back at the top of the stairs clutching backpacks stuffed with the items he'd told Lucy to gather. He hoped the adventure story he was reading at the moment had got it right and that was all they'd need. It had said something about ginger beer and ham. He didn't think Rosie had those things but they'd sneak into the kitchen and take whatever was easy to grab.

They crept down the stairs with Charlie leading the way. Lucy was too nervous to notice that she was following instead of leading.

In the dark, Rosie's house was lit up like the proverbial Christmas tree, lights shining from every window. Nick could see it as he turned the corner even though he was halfway down the street, but he was closer before he saw the police car parked out the front.

Pulling to a stop, in seconds he was knocking on her front door, heart pounding. He'd come with a plan to win back Rosie but what had he walked into? What was going on?

He knocked until the door swung open and immediately the adrenalin that had spurred him to come here tonight drained away.

He was face to face with Philip. Rosie's ex. Or was he no longer the ex? Was that why he was here?

Fighting every instinct to slug the guy, Nick stuck out his hand. 'Nick Masters.'

Philip returned the handshake. On reflection, Philip didn't look like the victor here, he looked exhausted and simply said, free of all bravado, 'You're Rosie's friend, Charlie's specialist.' Friend, doctor. That about covered what he was to Rosie, all right.

Nick motioned to the police car. 'Is everything okay?'

'You'd better talk to Rosie, not me.' Philip held the door wider, letting Nick enter before leading him through to the back of the house. Rosie was sitting white-faced on the family-room couch, two police officers sitting in chairs opposite her. At the sight, Nick's insides clenched and he went cold all over. Self-indulgent, uncharitable thoughts about Philip slid away in a moment. This didn't look good.

'Rosie, what's happened?'

She stood up the moment she saw it was him and crossed the room, placing her hands on his chest and standing close as she looked into his eyes, her gaze stricken. It was automatic to wrap her in his arms, hold her close.

'The twins have gone. You haven't heard from them, have you, Nick?' Her voice caught on a sob.

He shook his head and the police officers stood, obviously figuring Nick didn't have any information. The female officer handed Rosie a piece of paper and said, 'We'll keep you informed. Here's my mobile number. Ring me direct if they come home.'

Philip showed the officers out, leaving Nick and Rosie alone.

He relaxed his hold on her, moving back slightly so he could study her face, which he saw now was ashen and tear-stained. 'How long have they been missing?'

'I'm not sure. Philip arrived about five o'clock, the twins were eating dinner. He wanted to talk to me and the twins were keen to go and get ready for bed.' Nick heard the front door close, heard Philip's footsteps coming down the hall. Rosie had her arms folded across her chest, almost wrapping them around herself, her face tear-streaked, her eyes red from crying. 'I went up and kissed them later, about sixish. They said they didn't want stories, they wanted to just read in their own beds. I knew they were very tired, so I didn't think anything of it.'

As Philip came back into the room Rosie moved away from Nick, back to her seat on the couch. Nick wanted to sit beside her, to offer comfort, but he still wasn't sure what Philip was doing there. He sat in one of the chairs vacated by the police officers instead. Philip sat in the other, both of them facing Rosie. Nick fought off the feeling that the two men were in some sort of competition, both vying for Rosie's affections. This wasn't the moment to be thinking those thoughts.

Rosie continued. 'It was another half an hour before I went up to check on them again and they were gone. They've taken their backpacks.' He knew instinctively from the way her throat was working that she was fighting to stem her tears. 'I think they've taken food.'

'You didn't hear them come downstairs?'

'No, we were in the lounge at the front of the house.'

The more private area of the house, he knew that. What had they been discussing that had needed privacy? He bit his tongue, holding back the question. 'So they've been missing for anywhere up to an hour and a half. And you've got no idea where they might have gone.'

She shook her head. 'I've been trying to ring you to see if you'd heard from them, I know it's unlikely but the police said try everyone, so we have been.' Again she glanced at Philip, who nodded. 'Your office was closed, your private office line was engaged and your mobile was going to message bank.'

He cursed and pulled his phone from his pocket. He'd switched it off again after talking to his mum and he hadn't checked for any other messages, hadn't thought of anything but getting back to Rosie. 'Your parents haven't seen them?' A futile question. Of course she would have checked.

'Dad's out driving, looking for them, school friends are doing the same and Mum is at home, waiting, like we are...' she nodded at Philip '...in case...' She stopped herself and said instead, 'For them to come home.'

He'd come here intending to fight for Rosie but he hadn't expected to find Philip here. He couldn't help his blood running cold when Rosie spoke of herself and Philip as 'we'. Why was he here? Had she rung him to be her support? Where had he come from? He couldn't have got here so quickly from Canberra. But those questions would have to wait. Everything would have to wait until Lucy and Charlie were found. That was now the only issue.

'You've got no idea why they ran off?'

Rosie looked embarrassed, glancing at Philip before shaking her head. 'No, not really.'

Something was going on and it involved Philip. He waited for her to explain further but there was only silence.

'What would you like me to do?' He was already standing. He knew he couldn't stay and the only thing he could think about doing was searching for the twins. But part of him was hoping she'd ask him to stay. And tell Philip to go. 'What can I do?'

Rosie didn't quite meet his eye and she looked awkward as she said, 'Drive and look for them?'

He didn't trust himself to say much, just shoved his hands deep in his pockets, nodded and said, 'I'll see myself out. Let me know—'

She didn't let him finish, seeming anxious not to hear his words. 'I will.'

Despite burning with the feeling he'd just been dismissed, his overriding concern was for the twins. 'We'll find them, Rosie, they'll be okay.'

Rosie's bottom lip wobbled and a tear balanced on her lower

lash. It took all his strength to leave her there, to leave her with Philip, but the only thing that mattered now was finding the twins. And finding them safe.

Four hours later, Nick was still driving the streets of Bondi. He'd gone home twice, briefly, just to check, just in case, but neither time had there been any sign of the children. It was late, nearly midnight. The streets of Bondi were no place for eight-year-olds at that time of night. The thought of the twins being out amongst the crowds of drunken party-goers made him feel sick with fear. Where were they? His mobile had remained ominously silent on the car seat next to him.

He'd stay out all night if he had to. He didn't want to think about what would happen if they didn't find Lucy and Charlie tonight. Even thinking about what Philip might be doing at Rosie's was preferable but he didn't want to think about that either. He cruised around, peering down alleyways, automatically looking in whichever direction there was movement, but he saw nothing other than dishevelled adults.

Just after midnight, his mobile rang, the screen showing it was a private call.

He pulled over and snatched it up. 'Yes?'

'It's Rosie.'

'Where are you? Your number didn't come up. Do you know something?'

'No, I'm at home. I'm just using Philip's phone.' The jealousy in his gut tensed his stomach muscles into figures of eight. 'I want to leave my house phone and mobile free. You haven't seen anything?'

'No.' He hated thinking how she must be feeling right now. He felt sicker than he ever had before. How much worse must she feel? It was close to unbearable, not being able to do anything, other than this futile driving. 'I'll ring you when I find them.'

'I know but I had to check. I have to do something.'

In the background he heard Philip talking to her and knew she'd put her hand over the receiver to answer him. Jealousy clasped cold fingers around his heart and made him ask, 'Have you told the police everything?'

'What do you mean?'

He'd offended her. Tough luck. The question had to be asked. 'I'm not asking you to explain to me, but have you explained everything to the police? Told them everything that happened in the lead-up to the twins running away?' He couldn't bring himself to ask directly about why Philip was there, what they'd been discussing. He knew he'd find out later and until then he'd hope it was an explanation he'd be able to handle.

'I've told them everything I can remotely recall, no matter how unimportant I think it is. I'm not hiding anything from them.' Maybe not from the police but he knew he didn't yet have the whole story. He swallowed the words, repeating his mantra from tonight: now isn't the time.

'I'd better go, I want to keep looking.'

'Thank you, Nick, for helping, despite everything,' she said as she ended the call.

'Despite everything.' He damn well wished he knew exactly what she'd meant by that, just how many insults it covered. He pulled into another fast-food drive-through, bought his third tasteless cup of coffee for the night and downed the lukewarm liquid in a few gulps. He was close to home, he'd swing by once more.

Just in case.

'Someone's coming.' Charlie grabbed Lucy by the hand and tugged her away from the window and deeper into the shed. He flicked off his torch. They were plunged into almost total darkness, the streetlights scarcely penetrating the tiny louvred window.

In the blackness, two little hands found each other and held tight. Two little hearts pounded in unison and the silence was broken only by shallow breaths coming hard and fast.

Charlie knew now he only liked adventure stories in books. In reality, it had stopped being exciting hours ago. Now he was simply scared.

Nick was sure there had been a flash of light in his back garden. He locked his car and crept down the driveway, hugging close to the side of the house to avoid setting off the sensor light.

At the rear corner of the house he stood without moving, aiming to blend into the shape of the building. He let his eyes adjust to the darkness then scanned the garden. Shapes so familiar in the daylight took longer to identify now, but he knew something wasn't right.

His gaze moved slowly over the shed and on to the few old fruit trees in the rear corner, before shifting back to the shed. Something was wrong there, but what? He scanned the shed once, twice, and then he saw what it was. At the base of the shed window was a large piece of firewood standing on end like a seat. Or a stool. That hadn't been there before tonight. His eyes automatically checked the window. The pieces of glass from the louvre window had been removed. Had someone climbed into the locked shed? Was that someone still in there? Could it be the twins?

He stayed where he was, pressed against the house as he weighed up his next move. A sneeze broke the silence, then he heard a child's voice saying, 'Be quiet.'

Bingo. That was Charlie. He'd know that husky little voice anywhere; after the battle to get Charlie to talk in the first place, he wasn't likely to forget it. The relief he felt on finding them was enormous.

He covered the grass that lay between him and the shed in five long strides. 'Lucy, Charlie, don't be scared, it's Nick. Everything is okay.' From inside, there was a single sharp sob and then silence. Nick continued to talk as he pulled out his keys and fiddled with the padlock on the shed door, a difficult task in the near darkness. Finally, the lock fell open and the door scraped on the cement footing as he pulled it outwards.

He'd expected to have to extract them from their hiding place but as the door opened a warm little body hurtled forward through the dark. His immediate thought was they were running again and he readied himself to grab them, but the child simply ran forward and fell into his arms. Little arms wrapped tight around his neck and the single sob became a torrent, his neck awash with tears. Lucy. A very frightened Lucy.

He held her tight, squatting on the ground with her, rocking her to and fro like a much smaller child while he muttered soothing sounds. All the while he listened and watched for Charlie, his mind consumed with fear over what had happened to make them run away. And, worse, what might have happened to them since then.

It seemed like for ever but eventually a little white face appeared in the doorway and Charlie crept forward. Nick reached out for him too and, just like Lucy, Charlie fell forward into his arms. A single choked sound escaped Charlie's lips and then the release came—Charlie's little body heaving as he sobbed. He was shaking so violently Nick had trouble holding on to him. Eventually his sobs subsided and he found his voice but his near hysterical babble froze Nick with its terror.

'Don't let her leave us, don't leave us, Rosie. We'll be good. Make her stay, make them come back. Mummy. Daddy. Rosie. Mummy. Daddy.' His words were punctuated with big gulps of air. 'Mummy, Mummy, Mummy.'

What the hell had happened?

CHAPTER ELEVEN

THE call had come through well after midnight.

'I have them, I'm bringing them home, they're okay.' She didn't recall what Nick had said other than that. She didn't know how she'd filled the minutes until he'd pulled up outside and she'd run to the car to gather her babies into her arms.

The moment after Nick had rung, once she'd known the children were fine, she'd convinced Philip to go to the hotel he stayed at on work trips and not crash on the couch. She'd have asked him to go before, but there had been no point in him driving around looking for the twins. He didn't know the area, and she'd have gone crazy with no company. But if the children had come home and seen him, who knew what would have happened next?

They had run away because of Philip. She wasn't sure of the exact reasons but she knew it was about him. Him and her. She'd managed to hurt Lucy and Charlie. Again. But this time it had been enough to make them flee the home they loved into the city, alone, at night.

The irony was, she'd ended it with Nick thinking she had to, for the twins' sake, then had managed to make things far, far worse thanks to her handling of the situation with Philip, a man she didn't love. And when the twins were really at risk, it was Nick she knew she could count on. And she'd been right.

The man she most trusted to find Charlie and Lucy was also the only one she'd wanted by her side through the long, heart-wrenching wait but she couldn't have both. And now it was over, what did he think had been behind her decision to ask him to go while Philip stayed?

She supposed some hours had passed now, but she didn't know what time it was, except that the night must almost be over.

Lucy had been almost limp with exhaustion but unable to sleep. Charlie had been wound up tight, and wouldn't let her touch him. He'd only wanted Nick. Exhausted as she was, even she could see the irony in the situation. Her actions with Nick had started this whole train of events and now here was Charlie refusing her touch and wanting Nick.

In the end she'd had to call the GP to sedate the children. She hated to have it done but they'd been beside themselves with fear and relief, anger and exhaustion. She'd put them in her bed, tucked curled up with one another, and had sat with them until they were asleep.

She knew the police had been to interview Nick—the GP had told her they were downstairs when Nick let him in. She imagined the officers had gone now, but was almost beyond caring. The twins were home. They were safe. That was all that mattered.

It was all that mattered, but as she headed downstairs to lock up the house, she was consumed with hope Nick was still there. Wild hope, considering what he must be thinking, but with the twins home, she could no longer hold it together.

What she wanted was Nick.

She entered the kitchen and he stood up. He was here.

But was he here for her?

It had been difficult to piece together the children's move-ments since they'd run away but it seemed they'd been lucky. They'd been sufficiently frightened by whatever they'd seen on the streets of Bondi to flee to Nick's early on and nothing dangerous had befallen them.

Nick had carried Charlie, still clinging to him, upstairs. He'd changed the little boy and tucked him into Rosie's bed, all without exchanging a word with Rosie.

He'd waited downstairs while their GP had arrived and sedated them.

He'd waited while Rosie had sat with them until they'd gone to sleep.

He'd waited while the police had come and gone, and patiently given his statement.

It was hard—damn it, it was almost impossible—but he could see the need for patience.

But now no more.

He was through with waiting.

She was heading downstairs and as her footfall sounded on the boards he stood up. She came into the kitchen, her bottom lip wobbling as it had earlier but this time the tears fell and she stepped forward into his arms. He hadn't intended to reach for her. He'd wanted explanations, but the thought that she wanted him, that it was him who was still here, Philip nowhere to be seen, was enough.

For now.

But not for ever.

She was clinging to him, holding him tight, and he was returning the embrace, pressing her against his chest, stroking her hair from her face. She was shaking and every now and then her breath caught in her throat.

When she pulled away, she rubbed at her eyes and he realised she must be tired too because he was utterly exhausted.

'I'll head off, we both need some sleep.' It was nonsense. He knew sleep wouldn't come easily, for him at least.

'Don't.' She grabbed his hand, swaying slightly on her feet. 'Stay. I need to talk to you, before the twins wake up tomorrow.'

She looked at the kitchen clock, which showed it was past four in the morning and shook her head. 'Today, I mean. Later today.'

'You need to get to bed, you look ready to fall over. But if you want to talk, tell me why they ran away. The truth, Rosie.' He fixed her with a look that challenged her to try any other sort of explanation. 'I know something is going on with you and Philip and I know that's why the children left. Charlie kept begging me to make you stay, promising he'd be good. He was near hysterical but that was clear enough. Where does he think you're going? Why does he think you'd leave them behind?'

'Philip asked me to move back to Canberra.'

He sat down on a kitchen chair. He'd known it was something like that, but hearing it from her was different.

'Because?' His voice was harsh, foreign even to his own ears.

She started to sit, too, then seemed to think better of it and stood behind her chair, holding on to its back, shifting from foot to foot as though standing still wasn't possible. 'He seemed to think we could all benefit from the move.'

'Does this have something to do with his promotion to Minister for Family Services?'

'You know about that?'

'I read the papers.' He paused. 'You said no, right? The twins misheard.'

'I don't know what they heard but—'

'You didn't say no?' The desperate cold fear that had been squeezing his heart all night tightened its grip once more. 'You're considering it?'

'No.' She shook her head, her eyes red and wild, begging him to listen. 'I knew I wasn't going back but for one mad moment I did consider it. Not for me, like I said, it was madness.'

'You considered it for Philip's sake?' Anger and jealousy rolled around in his gut, making him feel ill.

'Of course I didn't consider it for Philip. You think I'd move us all to Canberra just to help his *career*? How stupid do you think I am?'

He didn't answer, simply stared at her and didn't try to hide the fury burning inside him.

'I considered it for the twins.'

He opened his mouth to tell her she was making no sense, as the twins didn't even like Philip. She beat him to it.

'The twins need stability and security and if I can give it to them, I will. I know in my heart that Canberra—and Philip—wouldn't give them that but I doubt myself now. After the mess I made of everything when I kissed you, I doubt my judgement. That's why I wanted to make sure I was weighing things up properly. It took less than a second to know moving to Canberra is the last thing the twins need. They need Philip even less. But Charlie must have heard the beginning of the conversation and not the end.'

Nick didn't care about the sequence of events, what he cared about was the fact she'd thought Philip's proposition over in the first place. 'You thought about Philip's offer because of security and stability.' She nodded. Hesitantly, but it was confirmation all the same. It made a mockery of the declaration he'd made, of his feelings for her. 'I made you an offer, too, Rosie. I told you I wanted the whole deal, that I love you. You didn't give *that* any consideration at all.' He wanted to lash out, to hit something in frustration. 'Either you don't feel the same about me or you didn't think I could provide for you as well as Philip. Was it really the children stopping you from getting involved with me or was it because you'd never really ended it with Philip? Is he a better bet financially?'

'How can you even ask that? You know it was because of the children. Charlie was so upset he'd stopped talking. I had to do what I did.' She stopped, looking confused. He refused to share her confusion, it was all clear to him. He remained silent, fixed in a stubborn refusal to make this any easier on her than it was for him. She blinked, rubbed at the corner of her eye and went on, 'At least, I thought I did. But are you really saying you think I'd assess a relationship based on who could provide best financially? If you think that, then you don't get me.' Her voice was anguished, not angry, but he hardened his heart. 'Not at all.'

'That's the first thing we've agreed on for some time.' He pushed back, stood and swung the chair back into place under the table. 'I'm glad the twins are home safely. Perhaps in the future you can watch what you talk about when they're around.'

It was a cheap shot, a throw-away line laying blame for the twins' actions entirely at her feet. It was unfair and in saying it, he knew he'd shown himself to be bitter and angry. Damn it, he *was* bitter and angry and he could toss in disillusioned and devastated for good measure.

He'd regret his comment later. In fact, as he saw Rosie's shocked face drain of all remaining colour at his words, he almost regretted it right now, despite his black despair.

Almost.

But not quite.

Nick raised his glass in a toast as the impromptu speech by one of his partners came to an end. Looking around the table at the assembled company of his medical partners, celebrating at their annual practice dinner, it occurred to him this was as close as he came to having family in Australia. A nice group, sure, but was this what it had all been for?

At his belt, his mobile vibrated. Grabbing it, he checked the display. James. A strange time for him to ring.

Nodding his excuses, he left the restaurant, heading for the night air.

He answered the call. 'Mate, what's up?'

'A lot. I'm getting married.'

Nick stood gaping. Finally, he got it together enough to say, 'What do you mean? *Married* married?'

'What other sort is there?' James chuckled, clearly in the best of moods. 'It's Lettie, the girl I've been pining after for years. The timing was never right for us to get together so when it finally was, it all fell into place quickly. Turns out she felt the same all along.'

'You've wanted to be *married* all these bachelor years? What happened to your claims that work was all you needed, work and a few dalliances on the side?'

'That was all I needed while I waited for the woman I wanted. The marriage part I didn't know about until we were together, then it all became clear. I wanted to tell you the news personally, I've only just left her parents' house, we've been celebrating. Thought I'd keep celebrating over the phone with you.'

They talked some more about his fiancée and about the wedding, Nick, trying to adjust to the news, still being genuinely pleased to accept James's invitation to be best man.

'And you, what's up? Broken any vows? Still in over your head with your complicated girl? Where are you now with all that?'

Where was he? Funny, that was the question he'd been asking himself just as James had rung. He didn't give the answer that sprang readily to his lips: that it had all come undone in a mind-blowing fashion with his 'complicated girl'. That although he thought he understood why she'd considered Philip's offer, however briefly, and although he no longer even blamed her for it, the damage had been done. She'd considered another man's offer and turned his, Nick's, down.

There was really no going back from there.

He didn't say any of that. Instead, he gave the answer he should be elated by, but which left him feeling strangely flat. 'I'm where I wanted to be.' He filled James in on how the partnership issues had resolved.

'You don't sound too happy about it.'

He'd clawed his way here from the depths of near bankruptcy. Sweat, toil, sacrifice—that had been his catch-cry. What wasn't there to be happy about?

'And,' continued James, 'you didn't answer me about your complicated girl.'

'It'd take too long and I've got a dinner to get back to.'

'I take it from that all is not well on the love front. So tell me, you've got to where you wanted to be and found it's lonely at the top?'

'I'm hardly at the top. Yet. But, yeah, all it needs is hard work and focus, not miracles, and I'll get there.'

'But is it worth it? That's what you're asking yourself. No need to deny or confirm, I know it is because you are exactly where I was a couple of years ago, so focused on my career path I didn't think what I was doing it for. Once the penny dropped, it took another long, lonely year and more before I got my girl.' There was a moment's pause before he added, 'You don't sound great, Nick, mate. Think it over. Are you sure whatever's happened can't be sorted?'

They ended the call then, Nick promising to make it over to Perth for the engagement party in two months' time.

He stood for a moment, absent-mindedly tapping his mobile against his leg as he looked out unseeingly across the quiet city street. Was it worth it? He hadn't stopped to think whether it would be lonely at the top. He knew now he'd make it, he didn't doubt that.

But what would be waiting for him when he got there?

Rosie and the children were still in the habit of heading to the beach on Sunday mornings, even though Nippers' season was finished. Ally had joined them today but although she and Rosie were power-walking, they had no chance of keeping up with the twins, who were racing ahead of them with their new puppy, Lolly. Both children were shrieking with laughter as Lolly ran circles around their ankles and Rosie smiled as she watched. Getting Lolly had been the only good idea she'd had in the last month since kissing Nick had sent them all hurtling towards this mess.

'It's been years since I saw this time of day unless I'd stayed up all night,' said Ally. 'Now here I am, exercising at the crack of dawn. Amazing what wanting to impress a man can do when the man is a personal trainer.'

Rosie laughed. 'It's eight o'clock, not exactly the crack of dawn, but it's nice to finally have you on a schedule that works with mine.'

'Talking about your schedule, when are you going to pencil in some time to look at some Internet dating sites? It's perfect for you. You can surf the web while the kids are asleep, no need for a babysitter.'

'Thanks for the tip but—'

Ally held up her hands but didn't break stride. 'I know, I know, you only want Nick. I can't count how many times I've heard you say that over the past fortnight but what are you planning to do about it? I think it's time you stopped wallowing in self-pity.'

'I'm not—'

'Yes, you are. You're sitting around pining, hoping he's going to come begging. But as far as he's concerned, you dumped him, saying it was for the twins' sake, but you were still prepared to consider Philip's offer. I know, I know.' Ally held up a hand to stall Rosie's protest. 'You didn't really consider it, but he doesn't know that.' Ally was puffing now but obviously that wasn't going to stop her. 'I hate to be the one to tell you this but if there's any begging to be done, it'll have to be done by you. Besides, you can't use the twins as an excuse any more, they're both doing great.'

Ally was right. Rosie looked ahead to the twins, now

tumbling on the sand with Lolly. That was the bright spot in the mess she'd made. Charlie and Lucy were doing well. Once she'd convinced them none of them were leaving Sydney and she was not getting back with Philip, things had steadily improved. Charlie was talking to her again, as if nothing had ever happened. He was even talking to Ally and occasionally answered other adults when they addressed him.

They'd turned out to be a lot more resilient than she'd realised, just like Nick had suggested all those weeks ago. To a passer-by, they'd seem like normal, happy kids. And then she realised something: they *were* normal, happy kids.

And normal, happy kids didn't need her to sacrifice her own happiness for no good reason.

An image of her future appeared in her mind's eye, the future she wanted rather than the future she was looking at now. She sighed out loud. The chances of anything changing were highly unlikely.

'What is it?' Ally wanted to know.

'What's the point in begging? Why would he give me another chance?' She shuddered as she recalled how badly she'd handled the evening of the twins' disappearance. 'I wouldn't.'

'Rubbish. All you did was put the twins first, there's no harm in that. If he's half the man you've led me to believe he is, he'll understand. What he shouldn't put up with is you giving him the run-around. Talk to him, explain what happened. You're a good person, you deserve to be happy. What's the worst that can happen?' She wagged a finger at Rosie. 'And I've just thought of another thing, maybe the biggest thing.' She stressed the last two words. 'I think you gave up Nick exactly because you were in love with him, and you thought denying yourself was part of looking out for the twins.'

Had she?

'I always said,' continued Ally, 'your over-baked need to put everyone else first would get you nowhere.'

Was that what she'd done?

She thought it over. It was so simple it made perfect sense. She'd thought she was putting the twins first by ending things with Nick. Now they were coping better than she was. Had her refusal to factor her own needs and wants into her decisions brought them all dangerously close to disaster?

If she'd used some of Ally's simple logic weeks ago, they would surely have avoided at least some of the later, horrid events. She'd taken something that could have been quite simple and stirred it into a horrible, complicated mess. To a large degree because of her entrenched habit of putting herself last.

Selflessness the road to self-destruction? It was sure looking that way now.

'Ally?'

'You want that website address?'

Rosie gave her a little shove. 'No, I'm wondering if you can do me a favour.'

Ally listened, her grin widening as Rosie explained. When she'd finished Ally gave her a quick hug before cupping her hands around her mouth and yelling to the children, 'Last one to the point is a rotten egg.'

And the last Rosie saw was Ally, the children and one over-excited puppy, sprinting towards the far end of the beach. The sound of their squeals followed her from the beach and it felt like they were wishing her luck.

She wished she didn't need it.

But she knew how much she did.

CHAPTER TWELVE

IT WAS rare for Nick to sleep in but according to his watch it was almost nine o'clock. He rolled over and pulled the pillow over his head to block out the pounding. He should have refused that last brandy at last night's practice dinner. And he shouldn't have stayed out so damn late trying to act like he was on top of the world and disprove James's comment that he wasn't doing so great. Not when he hadn't had a decent night's sleep in weeks. Still, he hadn't overindulged so it was strange to have this pounding sensation.

It finally twigged. The banging wasn't in his head, someone was knocking on the front door. Easing out of bed, he threw on an old pair of shorts, and, still wiping a hand over his face to wake himself up, he pulled open the door, blinking in the morning sun.

When he saw who it was he blinked again, but she didn't disappear so it seemed he was awake, not dreaming.

Rosie.

He might have said her name out loud, he wasn't sure. She might have said his name, he really didn't know. All he knew was it was Rosie, long after he'd given up hope of seeing her again.

God, she was beautiful. He'd been trying to forget that, but here she was, proof positive. She was beautiful and apparently she was nervous. She was chewing on her lower lip and shifting from foot to foot as she stood on his front doorstep. Time stood still, as though they existed in a time warp. They were motionless, enchanted, and for a single long moment he simply looked at her.

'I…' She stopped, swallowed and started again. 'Would you like to walk to the beach and have one of these?' She was holding two paper cups of coffee, and held one out to him. 'With me?' She added the rider tentatively, as if it might be the thing that made him refuse.

He took the cup and met her gaze. She didn't look away, although a hint of red coloured her cheeks. At this point he had no idea why she was there. He had no clue. But it didn't matter. None of that was important. He'd figure it out later. He grabbed his keys, his sunglasses and a T-shirt that was flung over a chair in the hall and pulled the door shut behind him.

'Where are the children?'

'At the beach with my friend Ally.'

The girl from the gallery, he remembered her. Rosie didn't speak again until they arrived at the beach, although she sent frequent glances his way. They sat on the sand and Nick had a brief flashback to the day he'd met her. It seemed a lifetime ago.

He drained his coffee in one long gulp then sat back, shoving his hands behind him to support his weight. It was killing him to wait, wondering why Rosie had turned up, but he stretched out his legs and dug his toes into the sand, raised his face to the sky and shut his eyes as he drank in the warmth, pretending he had all the time in the world. It was killing him but a man had his pride and he wasn't about to beg for details.

She sat beside him. Hiding behind her sunglasses, she faced the water, not him. 'I owe you an apology.'

She took a deep breath. 'That night,' she began, 'when the twins ran away, everything came crashing down. I got everything wrong, every last thing. And most of all I let you leave without making you understand what had happened. I didn't think I deserved a chance to explain.'

'I'm listening now.' He heard the challenge in his voice. He was listening, but would what she said be worth hearing?

'You were right, I was careless. Charlie and Lucy overheard part of my conversation with Philip. They jumped to the conclusion I was going to move to Canberra but they also concluded that I was leaving them behind. They thought if they ran away I wouldn't be able to leave. I'd have to stay and find them.' Just the mention of Philip's name got his jealousy boiling again but he kept quiet. He'd hear her out.

'It was the same thing that was bothering them when Charlie saw you and I kissing.'

A dark pink flush covered her cheeks, camouflaging her freckles. She'd never looked more gorgeous. He steeled his heart. She hadn't said anything that changed anything. Not yet.

'They were terrified I'd leave them. They thought we'd be like their parents, go away together, without them, and not come back. And you were right about other things as well.'

'Yes?' He was having trouble focusing now she'd reminded him of the night they'd kissed and all those sensations came flooding back. The image was vivid. And distracting.

'I did, very briefly, consider Philip's suggestion because he could offer us stability. Not in a financial sense, it was never about that, but I'd managed to convince myself it was my duty to give the twins back as much as I could of what they'd lost. Including a family. I thought doing the right thing by the twins meant denying my own needs, like that would prove I was doing a good job as their guardian. I think I let you go in part to prove that. That because I wanted you so much, I shouldn't have you. And since I didn't want Philip, I thought I should think about his proposal, like the mere fact I wasn't interested myself must mean it was the right thing for the twins.'

She threw her sunglasses down onto the sand and swivelled until she was facing him, her legs tucked under her, her face anguished, her hands clenched together. 'I know, it sounds mad. It was mad, all of it. It made no sense. Even if I was going to sacrifice my own happiness for the children, being with Philip would never have been the right thing. He doesn't love the children. They don't love him. And neither do I. It was never about that.'

She searched his face for a reaction and with difficulty he remained impassive. She went on. 'I still can't believe all the trouble I created just by considering that option for a millisecond.' She shuddered. 'I still can't bear to think what might have happened if the twins hadn't known where you lived, if you hadn't found them.'

'And now?' He believed her. Crazy as her explanation was, he believed her, but did it make any difference? She hadn't thought what he was offering was worth fighting for. He bit back the retort. Patience was what was needed. He needed to hear her out. And then make up his mind. 'It's been a couple of weeks, Rosie. Why the delay, if you wanted to explain? To apologise?'

'I...' She swallowed, glanced away and then knelt up on the sand, slipping her sunglasses onto the top of her head and sliding his from his face so she could look into his eyes. 'The story of my life. I didn't think I deserved the chance. I'd made such a mess of it all. I made my niece and nephew so terrified and insecure they ran away. I drove you away because I convinced myself I didn't deserve to be happy when the twins had suffered so much.'

'Yet you're here now. What's changed?'

'Put simply, Ally helped me see today that's nonsense. She said I'm so used to putting myself second, it was easier to keep doing that than accept the challenge of giving myself some priority.'

He hadn't thought of that but the explanation fit what he knew about her, fitted what had happened. The shroud of rejection and hurt evaporated from around him but he couldn't act on that. Not yet. There was more he needed to hear. Knowing she was what he wanted, needed, wasn't enough. He needed to know she really believed in them, needed to be sure she knew she was entitled to the sort of happiness he wanted to bring her.

'What else did she say?'

'That I was making excuses so I could avoid dealing with the real issue. And she made me see clearly how well the twins are doing now and take some credit for it. Watching them today, I suddenly realised they're much happier than I am.'

'So they've bounced back.' Quicker than us, he could have added but restrained himself. She didn't need to know he'd had insomnia ever since they'd parted and it had got worse since that night the twins had disappeared. Work had been his only saviour and last night it had ceased to even be that. Once he'd finally known that was all there was for him, he'd never felt more dismal.

'But they're missing you. As soon as they believed I wasn't going anywhere, that we're staying in Sydney for good, all their angst surrounding you disappeared. Now I get a daily inquisition over why you don't come around any more.'

'What do you tell them?'

'I say I made a mistake and I hurt you. They tell me to say sorry and we can be friends again. Up until today I didn't think that could happen. I've made such a mess of things.'

'It has been that.'

'But according to Ally, it doesn't have to be.'

'What does she suggest?' Nick asked curiously.

'Actually, she thinks I should go online and find someone.'

'She does, does she?' He had a few words to say to Ally!

'But she says not to expect miracles online. And it's a miracle I'm after.'

'Miracles? What sort are we talking?'

'The happy-ever-after sort.'

'From what I've seen of the Internet, I agree with Ally. Expecting miracles is a tall order.'

'You've been looking for someone?' She sounded aghast.

For a brief moment he considered leading her further down that path, making her suffer like he'd suffered, but lying wasn't his style and neither was being mean. 'No.' He was gratified when she exhaled the breath she'd clearly been holding, waiting for his answer. 'But I've had a bit of time on my hands lately, since I became part of a couple and then single again all in the same night. The Internet has been a handy time-killer but mostly I've been looking for the best deal on importing Perky Nanas.'

She was watching him through narrowed eyes. 'Truly?'

He drew the shape of a cross over his chest. 'Truly. I'll give you a tip. For free.'

'Yes?' She was looking at him, eyes wide, lips parted, face full of hope. He resisted the urge to reach out and touch her freckles. There were still things to be said and he knew touching her would mean the end of talking.

'Advertising locally is the safer bet. Try it.'

'Here?'

He shrugged. 'Couldn't hurt.'

She cleared her throat, sending him a slightly embarrassed glance before saying, 'Unemployed female doctor—'

'Hold it. So you really have quit your job?'

She nodded. 'The day after the twins ran away. There was never really any doubt about it, I just needed a little push to make the break.'

So far, this ad was looking okay. 'Go on.'

'Unemployed female doctor, new mother to two rapscallion children...' she was smiling now, warming up to the task '...seeks permanent partner, has to be a Kiwi, and a doctor, must like Sunday morning coffee by the beach, have a sweet tooth—'

'You do or he has to?'

'He has to. I have to watch my weight.' She frowned at him. 'I'm advertising for a man.' She bit down on her lip to keep from smiling. With difficulty, he kept a straight face, too.

'Fair enough.' He nodded. 'Keep going.'

'Must love children, puppies that chew everything in sight, and utter chaos in the morning. Must kiss like a bad boy and—' She stopped, apparently distracted by his mouth, which she appeared absorbed by.

'What? And he must what? After the kissing part.'

'I don't know what happens after the kissing part. That's why I need to find this man. The man I want did kiss me once, but we were fairly thoroughly interrupted. Nick?' She leant forward, her hand trailing down his cheek. 'I hate cliff-hangers. Would you mind very much if we found out how that kiss ended?'

'We can't.'

Shock filled her face. 'You don't want to?'

'I have to answer that ad first, before some other Kiwi sees it and responds.'

She nodded slowly and he noticed she had crossed her fingers on her right hand and was holding them tight.

'As far as the ad goes, yes, I'm interested. Yes, I fit the criteria but, like you said, there's one item we have to finish testing before I can give you my final answer.'

Her lips parted but it seemed she, too, was done with talking. She placed her hands on his chest and leant into him, her gaze roaming across his face before settling on his mouth. She leaned in a little more, her lips opened every so slightly. He pulled away and hauled her onto him, rolling over in one smooth movement so he had her lying on her back in the sand. The length of her toned body was moulded under his, skin against skin, where he'd wanted to be.

He'd never claimed to be a saint and right now all he wanted was the sinning.

Her hands threaded through his hair, and he breathed in the scent of her—roses, sunscreen and coffee. Looking deep into his eyes, he knew she'd never been more beautiful, her cheeks flushed, her pupils large and inky black. With a sound somewhere between a growl and a groan that expressed the anguish of these last weeks, he brought his mouth down to cover hers and kissed her with all the passion he'd been suppressing for so long.

When they finally came up for air she was grinning at him. Her hair had come loose from the constraints of its ponytail. She looked messy and lovely and pink and happy.

'So I guess now we know how the kiss ends. Does this mean you like my ad?'

'No, it's awful.' He grinned, sitting up and pulling her up with him. If he didn't sit up, he wouldn't be able to stop kissing her and there were still things that needed to be sorted. 'It needs to be withdrawn because you, Rosie Jefferson, are officially off the market.'

'You forgive me?' Her smile widened, transforming her face into a picture of unabashed, immeasurable happiness and loveliness.

'Yes, I forgive you for putting the children first. I'd expect nothing less from you. I even forgive you for putting me through hell. But only if, this time, when I tell you I love you, you don't push me away. Because I do love you, Rosie, and without you all my plans, all the work is meaningless. James asked me last night if it was lonely at the top.' He shuddered, remembering the last weeks of despair. 'I'm nowhere near the summit and already I'm miserable, wondering what it's all been for and knowing the answer can only be you.'

He wasn't sure but it looked like there were tears in Rosie's eyes as she searched for confirmation. 'Me?'

He nodded, reaching out to tuck some loose strands of blonde hair behind her ear. 'It's you, Rosie. It's been you since the moment you first smiled at me. You and those rapscallion children. I want to make a life with the three of you.'

Over Rosie's head he could see Ally and the twins making their way back up the beach towards them. He moved until he was kneeling up on one knee in front of her. 'I'd like to be able to give you a long speech right now but I reckon we have maybe fifty-five seconds until we're invaded. If it's all right with you, I'll give you the condensed version.' He took her hand in his. 'Rosie, let me love you. Let me adore you and cherish you.' Her eyes were wide as saucers and she was nodding mutely. 'Will you do me the honour of becoming my wife?'

She was nodding, smiling, her green eyes still dark with desire, her face aglow with surprise and pleasure. 'Yes, yes, to all of it. For the first time I can truly say I'm okay with someone doing things for me. I can't wait to be adored. And as for being cherished, yes, please.' Rosie took his other hand in hers too and clasped it tight. 'Nick, I've made every mistake I can think of and I'm sure I'll make many more. But I promise to never, ever doubt that you are the one I need. And love.'

He slid an arm behind her and leant her back until they were lying on the warm sand again. And this time there were no questions behind their kiss, there were only answers.

'Yuck!' said Charlie from somewhere above them. 'More kissing.'

Reluctantly, Nick ended the kiss and sat up, pulling Rosie up again but tucking her in against his side, where she belonged. He surveyed their company. They were surrounded by a grinning Ally, two bouncing children and a wet, sandy dog. 'Hello, there. I can see kissing Rosie will need some careful planning. Either that or I'll have to get used to an audience.'

'Does this mean you two have sorted out your differences?' Ally asked.

'What this means is that Rosie has agreed to marry me.'

'You're getting married!' Lucy clapped her hands together in excitement.

'But Rosie has one condition. You.' He grabbed Lucy and tugged her down onto their laps, touching the little girl on the tip of her nose. 'And you,' he said to a squealing Charlie as he pulled him, too, off his feet down on top of Rosie, Lucy and himself. 'And even that naughty puppy over there have to agree to live happily ever after, too. What do you say?'

The twins squealed with delight and promptly jumped up and down on top of Rosie and Nick. In perfect unison, they shouted, 'We say yes!'

His beautiful Rosie was laughing, and even with two small children using him as a trampoline, Nick couldn't wait any longer. He leant over, squashing the twins in the process, making them screech even louder, and kissed Rosie.

Because this was the time.

This was the place.

And this, most definitely, was the woman.

0709 Gen Std HB

ROMANCE

Desert Prince, Bride of Innocence	Lynne Graham
Raffaele: Taming His Tempestuous Virgin	Sandra Marton
The Italian Billionaire's Secretary Mistress	Sharon Kendrick
Bride, Bought and Paid For	Helen Bianchin
Hired for the Boss's Bedroom	Cathy Williams
The Christmas Love-Child	Jennie Lucas
Mistress to the Merciless Millionaire	Abby Green
Italian Boss, Proud Miss Prim	Susan Stephens
Proud Revenge, Passionate Wedlock	Janette Kenny
The Buenos Aires Marriage Deal	Maggie Cox
Betrothed: To the People's Prince	Marion Lennox
The Bridesmaid's Baby	Barbara Hannay
The Greek's Long-Lost Son	Rebecca Winters
His Housekeeper Bride	Melissa James
A Princess for Christmas	Shirley Jump
The Frenchman's Plain-Jane Project	Myrna Mackenzie
Italian Doctor, Dream Proposal	Margaret McDonagh
Marriage Reunited: Baby on the Way	Sharon Archer

HISTORICAL

The Brigadier's Daughter	Catherine March
The Wicked Baron	Sarah Mallory
His Runaway Maiden	June Francis

MEDICAL™

Wanted: A Father for her Twins	Emily Forbes
Bride on the Children's Ward	Lucy Clark
The Rebel of Penhally Bay	Caroline Anderson
Marrying the Playboy Doctor	Laura Iding

™ MILLS & BOON®

AUGUST 2009 LARGE PRINT TITLES

ROMANCE

The Spanish Billionaire's Pregnant Wife	Lynne Graham
The Italian's Ruthless Marriage Command	Helen Bianchin
The Brunelli Baby Bargain	Kim Lawrence
The French Tycoon's Pregnant Mistress	Abby Green
Diamond in the Rough	Diana Palmer
Secret Baby, Surprise Parents	Liz Fielding
The Rebel King	Melissa James
Nine-to-Five Bride	Jennie Adams

HISTORICAL

The Disgraceful Mr Ravenhurst	Louise Allen
The Duke's Cinderella Bride	Carole Mortimer
Impoverished Miss, Convenient Wife	Michelle Styles

MEDICAL™

Children's Doctor, Society Bride	Joanna Neil
The Heart Surgeon's Baby Surprise	Meredith Webber
A Wife for the Baby Doctor	Josie Metcalfe
The Royal Doctor's Bride	Jessica Matthews
Outback Doctor, English Bride	Leah Martyn
Surgeon Boss, Surprise Dad	Janice Lynn

0809 Gen Std HB

SEPTEMBER 2009 HARDBACK TITLES

ROMANCE

A Bride for His Majesty's Pleasure	Penny Jordan
The Master Player	Emma Darcy
The Infamous Italian's Secret Baby	Carole Mortimer
The Millionaire's Christmas Wife	Helen Brooks
Duty, Desire and the Desert King	Jane Porter
Royal Love-Child, Forbidden Marriage	Kate Hewitt
One-Night Mistress...Convenient Wife	Anne McAllister
Prince of Montéz, Pregnant Mistress	Sabrina Philips
The Count of Castelfino	Christina Hollis
Beauty and the Billionaire	Barbara Dunlop
Crowned: The Palace Nanny	Marion Lennox
Christmas Angel for the Billionaire	Liz Fielding
Under the Boss's Mistletoe	Jessica Hart
Jingle-Bell Baby	Linda Goodnight
The Magic of a Family Christmas	Susan Meier
Mistletoe & Marriage	Patricia Thayer & Donna Alward
Her Baby Out of the Blue	Alison Roberts
A Doctor, A Nurse: A Christmas Baby	Amy Andrews

HISTORICAL

Devilish Lord, Mysterious Miss	Annie Burrows
To Kiss a Count	Amanda McCabe
The Earl and the Governess	Sarah Elliott

MEDICAL™

Country Midwife, Christmas Bride	Abigail Gordon
Greek Doctor: One Magical Christmas	Meredith Webber
Spanish Doctor, Pregnant Midwife	Anne Fraser
Expecting a Christmas Miracle	Laura Iding

0809 Gen Std LP

MILLS & BOON®

SEPTEMBER 2009 LARGE PRINT TITLES

ROMANCE

The Sicilian Boss's Mistress	Penny Jordan
Pregnant with the Billionaire's Baby	Carole Mortimer
The Venadicci Marriage Vengeance	Melanie Milburne
The Ruthless Billionaire's Virgin	Susan Stephens
Italian Tycoon, Secret Son	Lucy Gordon
Adopted: Family in a Million	Barbara McMahon
The Billionaire's Baby	Nicola Marsh
Blind-Date Baby	Fiona Harper

HISTORICAL

Lord Braybrook's Penniless Bride	Elizabeth Rolls
A Country Miss in Hanover Square	Anne Herries
Chosen for the Marriage Bed	Anne O'Brien

MEDICAL™

The Children's Doctor's Special Proposal	Kate Hardy
English Doctor, Italian Bride	Carol Marinelli
The Doctor's Baby Bombshell	Jennifer Taylor
Emergency: Single Dad, Mother Needed	Laura Iding
The Doctor Claims His Bride	Fiona Lowe
Assignment: Baby	Lynne Marshall